IT'S A BEAUTIFUL DAY AT THE PLAZA

Story by and written by
Lydia Green & Liliane Pelzman

THE PRESENT - SANTA MONICA CALIFORNIA
EXT. BEACH - SUNRISE

It's a morning that explains why every person
lives in California. Spring is in full bloom, the
sun shines, the beach sand perfectly combed and
the sky is that perfect   blue.

MICHELLE THOMAS, (40's), strong, athletic and
good to look at, she's the epitome of 40's is the
new 30's runs along the waters edge. At station
24 she checks the time. It's 6:30 am, she has the
beach to herself. She takes off her running
shoes, checks one last time that she's alone,
whips off her running attire and dives naked over
the next crashing wave. She comes up smiling. Her
morning ritual, better than any cup of coffee.

INT. BEACH NEIGHBORHOOD - MORNING

Michelle walks towards her apartment building.
The neighborhood is beginning to wake up around
her. She stops at an ANGRY NEIGHBOR. He stands on
his doorstep, looking down at MARTHA, (70's)
she's homeless along with her TABBY CAT, Touli
and SMALL MUTT Georgie with only three legs. The
Angry Neighbor's doorstep was their bed for the
night.

> ANGRY NEIGHBOR
> (to Martha)
> I pay my taxes for what? For this?

Martha gets up, picks up her blanket, folding it
neatly and begins to walk away.

> ANGRY NEIGHBOR (CONT'D)
> You come back again, I'll have you
> and your animals arrested!

The Angry Neighbor goes back inside. Martha
drapes the cat over her shoulder and walks

towards the beach with the three legged dog at her feet.

> MICHELLE
> Hold on! Mam! I'll be right back!

Michelle runs up her apartment stairs and goes inside.

INT. MICHELLE'S APARTMENT - CONTINUOUS

Michelle grabs a loaf of bread, an orange, apple and a jar of peanut butter. Throws them in a bag and heads for the door.

EXT. BEACH NEIGHBORHOOD - CONTINUOUS

Michelle looks around. Martha is gone. Michelle runs with the bag towards the beach, she catches up with Martha.

> MICHELLE
> (holding out the bag)
> Take this. I'm sorry I have nothing for your animals.

Martha turns and smiles whole-heartedly through her tear stained face and missing teeth. She gratefully takes the bag.

> MARTHA
> Thank you. You are a dear.

Michelle pets the cat around Michelle's shoulders and crouches down to her dog.

> MICHELLE
> Cute little family you have here.

> MARTHA
> Touli and Georgie.

Martha begins to walk away. Michelle watches.

EXT. MICHELLE'S APARTMENT - MOMENTS LATER

Michelle opens her mailbox and collects her mail.
Looking through it, she opens a letter and walks
inside.

INT. MICHELLE'S APARTMENT - MOMENTS LATER

Michelle drops her mail on the counter and
continues reading the letter.

CLOSE UP OF LETTER READS WEST LA RETIREMENT
PLAZA. It's a notice of late payment.

Michelle notices her answering machine is
blinking, she presses the incoming message
button. She leans against the counter staring at
the letter, the stress of life showing in her
demeanor.

> CAPTAIN THOMAS (O.S.)
> This Pappa Alfa Zero Charlie India.
> This is an emergency. Communicate
> as soon as you can.

Michelle drops the letter on a stack of unpaid
bills, grabs the phone and dials.

> RETIREMENT RECEPTIONIST (O.S.)
> (cheery)
> The plaza. May I help you?

> MICHELLE
> Hi. Good morning. This is Michelle
> Thomas, the Captain's daughter.
> Room 214. He just left me another
> one of his emergency messages.

> RETIREMENT RECEPTIONIST (O.S.)
> He just signed out for his morning
> walk.

                    MICHELLE
                    (relieved)
         So he's okay. When he comes back
         in, please tell him I'll be there
           in a half hour, depending on
                     traffic.

Michelle hangs up and heads quickly towards the shower.

INT. THE WEST LOS ANGELES RETIREMENT PLAZA
LATER

A RECEPTIONIST smiles when Michelle enters. The phone RINGS at the same time.

                RETIREMENT RECEPTIONIST
                    (into phone)
           Good morning. The plaza. Hold one
                  minute please.
                   (to Michelle)
           Good morning Michelle. He just got
                 back from his walk.

Receptionist smiles at Michelle. Michelle signs in on the registry at the front desk.

            RETIREMENT RECEPTIONIST (CONT'D)
            Something's bugging him today.

Michelle smiles at her.

                    MICHELLE
           Thank you for the info.

Michelle heads to find her father.

INT. DINING ROOM - MOMENTS LATER - MORNING

The mood of the room feels antique. Breakfast has been cleared. A few ELDERLY sit at tables, staring into space waiting until they are told what to do next.

DAVID AND MARIE MIZRAHI (80's) hold each others hand across the table. Mr. Mizrahi has a Jewish Kippah on his head.

Michelle stops at their table.

> MICHELLE
> Good morning Mr. and Mrs. Mizrahi.
> Have you seen the Captain?

Mr. and Mrs. Mizrahi look up at Michelle with a smile.

> MARIE MIZRAHI
> (a revolution)
> Yes...Mizrahi, that's my name.
> (to her husband)
> Who are you?

Mr. Mizrahi takes a white handkerchief out of his pocket and wipes his wife's chin.

> MR. MIZRAHI
> Hello...Michelle. I think I saw the
> captain this morning. Yes...he was
> at breakfast--

> MRS. MIZRAHI
> (to her husband)
> My...you're a captain?

Mr. Mizrahi smiles patiently at his wife. Michelle realizes Mr. Mizrahi has his hands full.

> MICHELLE
> Thank you.

Michelle walks through a long corridor, apartments on either side. She stops at door "214" a sign above it reads "COCKPIT."

Michelle KNOCKS on the door and enters. Her father, CAPTAIN DONALD THOMAS (late 70's) is pacing back and forth. He wears a navy blue pilot captains hat, it's one of his possessions that reminds him he had a life before he moved into an assistant living facility.

> CAPTAIN THOMAS
> What took you so long?

Michelle understands him, she always takes too long. He motions his daughter to sit down. After a MOMENT.

> MICHELLE
> Dad...are you okay?

> CAPTAIN THOMAS
> He's...stolen my girl.

Michelle takes a MOMENT before answering.

> MICHELLE
> Who?

> CAPTAIN THOMAS
> Lila.

> MICHELLE
> Lila?

Captain Thomas grabs his daughters hand and leads her out of the room. He's taking her to the disaster.

INT. ACTIVITY LOUNGE - MORNING

Captain Thomas leads his daughter to the window. Looking out to the garden, the answer is right there in front of Michelle.

> CAPTAIN THOMAS
> The bastard blew in yesterday
> afternoon. White sails and all.

EXT. THE WEST LA RETIREMENT PLAZA - GARDEN

CAPTAIN ALBERT BROOKS (late 70's) stands in the gardens. He is dressed in white and wears a white cruise ship captains hat.

LILA (80's), her appearance is hidden behind a parasol, she stands with a cane. Captain Brooks seems to be charming her with a little melody.

INT. ACTIVITY LOUNGE

Michelle looks at her father with sympathy.

MICHELLE
Dad, how long has this thing with
Lila been going on?

CAPTAIN THOMAS
We've been having dinner together.

MICHELLE
And now she's your girl?

Captain Thomas nods "yes". He's smitten alright.

CAPTAIN THOMAS
I'll have to have a little talk
with this Captain. Find out his
intentions.

Michelle rolls her eyes.

MICHELLE
He's just enjoying her company.

CAPTAIN THOMAS
Affirmative! But you can't have two
Captains. It's a disaster!

Michelle thinks for a MOMENT.

MICHELLE
You haven't lost Lila dad. She's

just talking to Captain Whitey out
there.

CAPTAIN THOMAS
But she loves going on cruises.

MICHELLE
(trying to make light of
the situation)
She's not going anywhere very fast,
looks to me like she has a walking
cane.

CAPTAIN THOMAS
Not funny darling. The poor girl
has to have another hip replacement
and insurance keeps putting her off
because her surgery was less than
two years ago. I want to know what
he's singing to her.

MICHELLE
Dad...well...that would be a good
thing but I think your imagination--

CAPTAIN THOMAS
He comes sailing in here... Already
has a captains table in the dining
room.

MICHELLE
Wow...I like this guy already.

Captain Thomas isn't impressed with his
daughter's capacity of compassion at this moment.

MICHELLE (CONT'D)
Look...I'm late for work. I'll come
back tomorrow and we'll see if Lila
has decided if the cockpit is still
in favor over the bridge.

Michelle hugs and kisses her distraught father. She starts to walk away, but turns and looks lovingly at her father.

> MICHELLE (CONT'D)
> Dad...treat this like an
> ...airborne delay. Just a delay.
> We'll figure it out.

Michelle leaves her father peeking out at his view of doom.

DINING ROOM

Michelle passes Mr. and Mrs. Mizrahi still holding hands across the table. As Michelle passes...

> MICHELLE (CONT'D)
> Good bye you guys.

Mr. and Mrs. Mizrahi looks at each other.

> MR. MIZRAHI
> Who's that?

Mrs. Mizrahi shrugs her shoulders.

> MRS. MIZRAHI
> I've never seen this woman before.

Michelle leaves as the reception phone RINGS.

> RECEPTIONIST (O.S.)
> The plaza. Good morning.

EXT. WEST LOS ANGELES - WILSHIRE BLVD - LATER

Michelle sits in stop and go traffic. The light turns green but no one is moving. Car horns BLAST at the problem ahead. Michelle opens her window trying to get a view at what is causing the problem. Car HORNS BLAST adding to the tension.

CROSSWALK

HAROLD SANDERS (80-90's), American Indian, barefoot, homeless appearance is causing the problem today. Crossing at the light, something has fallen out of his pocket and he is frantically looking for it.

Michelle is out of her car, runs up to the mishap and helps look for whatever Harold has dropped.

Harold points to something under the car in front of him.

Horns continue to BLAST. Michelle turns and stares at the angry traffic. She puts her hands up as if to say "really people, is this what America has come too?"

CITY SILENCE. The traffic actually got her message.

Michelle gets down on her knees and reaches under the car. She returns with a PRAYER STICK. Feathers tied to a small stick wrapped in leather, Harold places it into his pocket.

                    MICHELLE
            That's a Native Indian prayer
                    stick.

Harold looks at her. He points to his right ear, he can't
hear a thing. He turns his left side of his face
                    to her.

                  MICHELLE (CONT'D)
            Be careful out here. It's a war
                    zone.

A toothless smile towards Michelle shows his gratitude and he quickly moves to the sidewalk.

11

Michelle walks quickly back to her car. And pulls ahead with the traffic.

INT. BANK OF AMERICA - LATER

Michelle enters the bank and heads directly to her desk.EMPLOYEES look up from their tellers. Michelle has been late for work for the past few months and we know why.

CHUCK HARRIS (40's) the Bank Manager, good looks and knows it, looks up from his glassed office. He's on his way over to Michelle before she can even open her computer.

Chuck sits on her desk, sitting on her hand, looking down at her. Michelle pulls her hand away quickly. Chuck smiles.

                    CHUCK HARRIS
            You get a good feel?

                    MICHELLE
        I got enough of a feel the first
                    time.

                    CHUCK HARRIS
            You don't want more?

Michelle ignores him, she's not discussing this any further.

                    MICHELLE
        The quarterly tax reports are on
                your desk.

Chuck continues to look down at her.

                    CHUCK HARRIS
        Who's going to get the President
            Club Award this year?

Michelle's eyes are glued to her computer.

                MICHELLE
Did you have a chance to check out
  the loan statements I gave you
           yesterday?

             CHUCK HARRIS
      Who are you taking?

Michelle smiles incredulously, stands and looks
at him straight in the eyes.

              MICHELLE
If you really need a holiday, I'd
be glad to give you and your wife
    the trip if I win it.

             CHUCK HARRIS
        Come on babe.

              MICHELLE
  No more babe. You lost that
privilege when I figured out you
   were playing both of us.

Michelle sits back down again.

             CHUCK HARRIS
  It was a little white lie.

              MICHELLE
  I don't do married men.

Chuck looks around before stepping in closer, his
crotch at Michelle's eye level.

             CHUCK HARRIS
   God I miss your smell.

Michelle knows what he's doing, her eyes glued to
her computer.

         CHUCK HARRIS (CONT'D)
   I'm not done with us yet.

Chuck begins to walk away.

MICHELLE
Yea...tell that to your fly.

Chuck stops, zips his fly and begins to walk back
to his glassed office. DELIA ZAMORA (60's) a
Spanish Woman, a enters the bank and intercepts
Chuck.

DELIA ZAMORA
Excuse me Senor. No hay ningun
dinero en la maquina. He intentado
retirar veinte dolares, pero la
maquina no me da el dinero.

Chuck barely gives her a MOMENT. He just points
in the direction of Michelle. Delia nervously
smiles and joins Michelle at her desk.

DELIA ZAMORA (CONT'D)
Excuse me Seorita. No hay ningun
dinero en la maquina. Creo que la
maquina se rompe. (No cash in the
machine. I think the machine is
broken.)

Michelle recognizes this customer from the day
before. Michelle's expression conveys she's in a
tough position with this situation.

MICHELLE
Hello...Hola, Ms. Zamora. Delia
Zamora?

DELIA ZAMORA
Si.

Michelle types the customers name into the
computer and reads the screen. Michelle turns the
computer around so Delia can see the screen.

MICHELLE
No creo que haya un problema con la

14

maquina. Su cuenta fue cerrada el
mes pasado debido a la falta de
fondos. (a beat) Lo Siento. There
is no problem with the machine.
Your account was closed last month
because of the lack of funds. I'm
sorry.

Delia stands.

DELIA ZAMORA
(angry)
No! Hay un problema con la maquina!

Michelle stands and walks towards the ATM located
outside the front door of the bank. Delia follows
close behind but Chuck approaches quickly.

CHUCK HARRIS
What seems to be the trouble?

MICHELLE
I can handle it. Our customer is in
a bad predicament here.

Chuck motions Michelle aside.

CHUCK HARRIS
What? Explain again to her like you
did yesterday that her account has
been overdrawn for the last three
months.

MICHELLE
Her account has been with this bank
for twenty years--

CHUCK HARRIS
But our customers are supposed to
have money Michelle, that's why
they call us a bank.

MICHELLE
I'll check the ATM, show her that

that it's working and maybe give
her a twenty from my own account to
help her out.

CHUCK HARRIS
She comes back tomorrow, we let
security handle the problem.

Michelle continues to walk outside, Delia
follows.

EXT. BANK OF AMERICA - CONTINUOUS

Michelle enters her debit card. Delia stands
behind her nervously. Michelle enters security
code.

MICHELLE
As you can see...the ATM is working
just fine. (La ATM parece estar
funcionando bien.)

Delia looks around nervously, she reaches into
her handbag, she places her hand inside her purse
as if she were going to pull out a gun. Delia
jumps back as Michelle turns around and holds out
a twenty and offers it to Delia. Delia almost
disappointingly accepts the money.

MICHELLE (CONT'D)
I'm sorry. It's not much but it's
something. I wish I could help you
more. (Siento. No es mucho pero es
algo. Me gustaria poder ayudarte
mas.)

DELIA ZAMORA
(perfect English)
Thank you, you're a kind woman.

Michelle is taken aback by Delia's perfect
English. Delia walks away.

EXT. BANK OF AMERICA - DAY

Michelle locks up the front door to the bank and walks to her car. She looks up and notices Chuck is leaning against her car. She opens the driver's door and gets in. Chuck jumps into the passenger seat. Michelle isn't pleased.

> CHUCK HARRIS
> Why are you doing this?

Michelle LAUGHS incredulously.

> MICHELLE
> Chuck, I'm not interested in
> fooling around with a married man.
> I can't be any more blunt than
> that.

> CHUCK HARRIS
> You still want me.

> MICHELLE
> Stop it, my mind isn't on that
> right now. I may not have a wife
> and kid to feed but I have a father
> that's going to be evicted if I can
> help him pay his bills. Don't you
> remember? I told you all that.

> CHUCK HARRIS
> Vaguely.

> MICHELLE
> The airline company went belly up
> and his pension plan was
> terminated. My parent's savings is
> gone and I'm buried with all the
> hospital bills when my mom died of
> cancer.

> CHUCK HARRIS
> Health care should pay for that.

                    MICHELLE
         It doesn't pay for everything
         Chuck. And it certainly doesn't pay
         for assisted living. I'm all my
         father has and it's up to me now to
         make sure my dad has the last few
         years of his life with a
         comfortable pillow under his head.

                    CHUCK HARRIS
         Shit... (a beat) Can we talk about
                    us now.

                    MICHELLE
         We work together. That's it.

                    CHUCK HARRIS
         But we make a good team.

Chuck puts his hand on her thigh, feeling the
skin on her legs.

                    MICHELLE
         I need to go now.

Chuck doesn't move his hand. Michelle looks at
him. She places her hand strongly on the horn. It
BLASTS through the parking lot.

                    CHUCK HARRIS
         Okay! Okay! Shhhh!!! Stop!

Michelle takes her hand off the horn.

                    CHUCK HARRIS (CONT'D)
         It's kind of sexy when you're
                    pissed off.

Michelle BLASTS the horn again. Chuck relents and
gets out. Michelle drives off.

EXT. GROCERY STORE PARKING LOT - LATER

Michelle gets out of her car and walks inside.

INT. GROCERY STORE - LATER

CLOSE UP OF AISLE SIGN - "10 items or less."

Michelle has a hand basketful of grocery items, including dry cat and dog food. She stands in a long line behind SHOPPERS.

VIRGINIA JONES (80's) is at the front of the line. Behind her is MEL BROOKS (50's), he's an all around good guy. Her purchases are totaled by the CASHIER. Virginia has counted three times through to make sure she hasn't gone against the system.

                    MEL BROOKS
                  (to Virginia)
        I think your good. Definitely less
                  than ten items.

Virginia looks up at Mel and smiles with a thank you.

                    CASHIER
        Do you have your savings card?

Virginia is scrounging through her purse. She's digging, the other Shoppers are starting to grow impatient.

                    VIRGINIA
        I don't think I ever got one of
                    those.

The Cashier places an application on the counter.

                    CASHIER
        You have to have a smart shopper
        card to get our daily savings.

19

Virginia is looking through her bag.

                    VIRGINIA
            I don't have a pen.

The Cashier places a pen on the counter.

                    CASHIER
        Just a name and email is fine.

                    VIRGINIA
            Why do I need an email?

The cashier takes the application back.

                    CASHIER
            You need an email--

Mel starts to search is wallet for his savings
card.

                    MEL BROOKS
        You know my father has never had an
              email address either.

Michelle steps in and gives her savings card to
the Cashier.

                    MICHELLE
              Swipe mine.

The Cashier takes Michelle's card, swipes it and
gives it back. Michelle stands back in line. Mel
smiles at her with an approving nod.

                    CASHIER
        That will be twenty-one dollars and
              ninety-eight cents.

Virginia is already looking through her purse for
something else. She brings out a pile of ripped
coupons. The other Shoppers are starting to shift

in their stance, letting everyone know they are more important than any one else in that line-up. Mel turns to observe the rest of the line and somewhat smiles at the situation, we've all seen this many times before.

Placing the coupons on the register counter, Virginia goes through them slowly before picking out all the right ones that will give her a better discount. After a MOMENT.

                    CASHIER (CONT'D)
          Ok, that brings your total now to
          eighteen dollars and five cents.

Virginia reaches into her purse and hands over a few bills. The Cashier counts the money.

                    CASHIER (CONT'D)
          Mam...there's only fourteen dollars
                       here.

Virginia starts to rummage through her purse, bringing out penny by penny and totaling it up on the counter. She makes a mistake and starts from the beginning.

                  DISGRUNTLED SHOPPER
          Hey lady, why don't you just put
          something back and get it tomorrow?

                     MEL BROOKS
                    (to cashier)
          How much does she owe?

                      CASHIER
          She owes another four dollars and--

Virginia looks down at her purchases.

CLOSE-UP OF PURCHASES - Toothpaste, fiber cereal, milk and "Depends" diapers for the elderly and a PEZ Candy.

Virginia turns to the other less patient Shoppers and lifts the toothpaste with almost a toothless smile.

                    VIRGINIA
          Would you want to put this back and
                lose any more of these?
                (lifting fiber cereal)
              Everyone needs to shit!
              (referring to cereal and
                    lifting milk)
          I tried it with water, but it's my
                    one luxury.
                (lifting Depends)
            We'd all be standing in my piss
            right now, I've been standing here
                  a long time too.

Virginia hesitates before placing the PEZ candy to the side. Michelle steps in.

                    MICHELLE
                    (to Mel)
              Here's a few dollars.

Michelle passes the PEZ candy to Virginia and Mel adds a few extra dollars from his wallet to the cashier.

                    VIRGINIA
              (to Michelle and Mel)
            Thank you. It's ...my grandson's
                    birthday.

Virginia takes her bag of purchases and turns to leave but stops and looks back at all the Shoppers.

                VIRGINIA (CONT'D)
            Enjoy it while you have it.

                Virginia leaves.

INT. MICHELLE'S APARTMENT - SUNSET

Michelle stands, looking out her window. She's eating a bowl of pasta, her first food of the day. The view is small but she's grateful.

EXT. MICHELLE'S VIEW - CONTINUOUS

The sun almost behind the horizon, Martha, the bag lady walks along the sidewalk with her three legged dog, Georgie at her feet and the cat, Touli draped over her shoulders.

EXT. MICHELLE'S APARTMENT - CONTINUOUS

Michelle stands at the front door and drops a pillow on her doorstep. Places the small bags of dog and cat food next to the pillow, she closes the door.

INT. MICHELLE'S APARTMENT - NEXT MORNING

Light coming in through the window, Michelle is on her way out the door in her running attire.

EXT. MICHELLE'S APARTMENT - CONTINUOUS

Opening the door, Martha sleeps curled up in a ball, her head on the pillow that Michelle left the night before, her animals barely stir from their sleep.

Martha sits up quickly.

> MICHELLE
> Take your time. I'm an early bird.

Michelle runs towards the beach. Martha watches her.

EXT. MICHELLE'S APARTMENT - LATER

Michelle returns from her run. Martha is gone. Walking up the few stairs that lead to her front door. Michelle notices her watering can is in a different place and her dying plants have been taken care of a bit and watered. The pillow is neatly placed on a chair on the front doorstep. Michelle leaves it there and enters her apartment.

INT. MICHELLE'S APARTMENT - MOMENTS LATER

Michelle grabs a glass of orange juice and lifts her cell phone. She has a message, of course. She presses her home answering machine at the same time.

> CELL PHONE MESSAGE (O.S.)
> (Captain Thomas voice)
> Mayday, Mayday, Mayday! Distress in
> the cockpit. Report immediately!

> ANSWERING MACHINE (O.S.)
> (Captain Thomas' voice)
> Michelle! Where are you?

Michelle let's out a big "here we go again" SIGH. She quickly heads to the shower.

INT. WEST LOS ANGELES RETIREMENT HOME - MORNING - LATER

Michelle enters. The Receptionist is on the phone. Taking the phone away from her ear.

> RETIREMENT RECEPTIONIST
> (into phone)
> The plaza. Can you hold please.
> (to Michelle)
> We've had a bit of a drama this
> morning--

Mel (from the grocery store) enters in a panic.

                    MEL BROOKS
          Good morning. I had a urgent
          message from my father, Captain
                    Brooks.

Michelle and Mel recognize each other.

               MEL BROOKS (CONT'D)
          Ah...grocery store?

                    MICHELLE
               Good morning.

The Receptionist points towards the living room.

               RETIREMENT RECEPTIONIST
          I'm glad you're here. Their in the
                 activity lounge.

Michelle and Mel sign in quickly and head towards
the dining room.

DINING ROOM

Only a few elderly sit eating their breakfast,
Michelle notices the Mizrahi's table is vacant.
Other tables remain untouched, breakfast waiting
to be eaten.

                    MICHELLE
          You have any idea what's going on.

                      MEL
          Your guess is as good as mine.

They continue through the dining room towards the
room.

               RETIREMENT HOME MANAGER (O.S.)
          Everyone needs to calm down. We
          will find her. Please make your way

                      25

into the dining area, breakfast is
waiting for all of you at your
tables.

                    CAPTAIN THOMAS (O.S.)
          Where is she? You're lying to us!

Michelle follows the argument which is coming
from the Activity Lounge.

ACTIVITY LOUNGE

Crowded with OLD AGE PENSIONERS, some with
wheelchairs, walkers and canes surround the
RETIREMENT HOME MANAGER (40's). Captain Thomas
(Michelle's dad in his navy blue pilot hat) and
Captain Brooks (in his white Captains hat) have
the Retirement Home Manager trapped inside their
circle. It's a double Captain interrogation.

                    CAPTAIN BROOKS
                (to Retirement Manager)
          Sailor, if you were on my ship,
          you'd be walking the gang plank!

Mr. and Mrs. Mizrahi grab Michelle and Mel by the
arm as they enter the room. They escort them to
the center of the mass group.

Captain Thomas and Captain Brooks immediately
move towards Michelle and Mel. They move in for a
secretive huddle with their kids.

As this happens, the Retirement Home Manager
tries to escape but the Old Age Pensioners moves
in closer. Wheelchairs and walkers make a mighty
barricade.

In a huddle...

                    MICHELLE
                  (whispering)
          Dad...what's going on?

                    CAPTAIN THOMAS
            She wasn't in her room this
                       morning.

Captain Brooks and his son Mel step in closer.

                     MEL BROOKS
                   (to Michelle)
           Ah...hi. Mel. Nice to formally meet
                        you.

            Michelle shakes Mel's hand.

                     MICHELLE
            Looks like we have more in common
                  then we thought.

Captain Brooks takes Michelle's hand and kisses
it.

                   CAPTAIN BROOKS
            Retired Captain Albert Brooks of
            the Carnival Cruise Enchantment.
                The pleasure is all mine.
                 (to Captain Thomas)
              Gorgeous girl. Doesn't look
                  anything like you.

                     MICHELLE
                (to Captain Brooks)
              Ah...nice to meet you.

Captain Thomas rolls his eyes, at the charmer of
the sea. Captain Thomas introduces himself to
Mel.

                   CAPTAIN THOMAS
                  (to Mel Brooks)
            Captain Donald Thomas. Retired
            Commercial airline pilot. ATP and
                   MPL certified.

                     MEL BROOKS
                (shaking Captain Thomas'

hand)
Nice to meet you Captain Thomas.
Now can you guys tell us what's
going on here?

CAPTAIN THOMAS
We have to find her.

MICHELLE AND MEL
...Who?

CAPTAIN THOMAS AND CAPTAIN BROOKS
Lila!

Retirement Home Manager steps in.

RETIREMENT HOME MANAGER
Mr. Thomas...Mr. Brooks--

CAPTAIN THOMAS AND CAPTAIN BROOKS
CAPTAIN!

RETIREMENT HOME MANAGER
Captain Thomas...Captain
Brooks...I'm sure I can explain
everything. Why don't we just move
along? Get everyone to breakfast
and I'd be happy to explain in a
private situation where your friend
might have gone.

MICHELLE
(trying to calm the
situation)
That sounds fair.

The two Captains look at each other for a MOMENT,
and then simultaneously nod in agreement.

NURSES that have been standing on the sidelines
move in to guide the Old Age Residents towards
the dining room.

Michelle, Mel and the two Captains follow the
Retirement Home Manager towards his office.

INT. RETIREMENT HOME OFFICE - CONTINUOUS

The two Captains place a chair for Michelle to
sit down, Mel stands with the Captains. The
Retirement Home Manager takes out a file and
opens it on his desk.

                    RETIREMENT HOME MANAGER
             Now...what seems to be the problem?

                          MICHELLE
             Well it's obvious what's wrong. It
              seems like everyone wants to know
                         were Lila is.

                    RETIREMENT HOME MANAGER
              According to our file, she left
                      yesterday evening.

Michelle, Mel and the two Captains expressions
convey "and we would like more information."

               RETIREMENT HOME MANAGER (CONT'D)
                  I'm not authorized to give
                information regarding other
                         patients,

                         MEL BROOKS
              She's not a patient, she's a
             resident and a close friend of the
                     two Captains here.

                        CAPTAIN BROOKS
             We aren't leaving until you tell us
                        where she is.

The Retirement Home Manager sits back in his
chair assessing the situation. The two Captains
start to pace back and forth.

SILENCE.

                    RETIREMENT HOME MANAGER
              Listen...I run a business here, not
                  non-profit organization.
              My job is to keep the beds filled
                  with people that can pay their
              bills. Three months ago we notified
              Lila's family regarding past due
                            fees--

                         MICHELLE
              So... they came and picked her up?

                    RETIREMENT HOME MANAGER
                      Not...exactly.

                      CAPTAIN BROOKS
              So what exactly did you do with
                           her?

                        MEL BROOKS
              Can you give us some kind of
              information... I'm already late for
                           work.

                         MICHELLE
                    Get used to it.

The Manager stands and starts to walk towards the
door.

                    RETIREMENT HOME MANAGER
                  Like I said...I'm not in any
              position to divulge information, I
                suggest we go back to the dining
                  room, breakfast is wait--

The two Captains move in, swiftly as if their
timing of self defense tactics have been well
rehearsed. Captain Thomas cranks the Managers arm
around his back as Captain Brooks shoots a quick
kick to the Managers knees. He's instantly
down on all fours, begging for mercy.

MICHELLE
Holy Shit!

MEL BROOKS
Where'd you Captain America's learn
that?

CAPTAIN BROOKS
No time for a stowaway.

CAPTAIN THOMAS
No time for a hijacker.

Captain Thomas continues to hold down the Manager
to the floor. Captain Brooks slowly gets down on
his knees (he's old remember and that last shin
kick maneuver tweaked his back a little)
Eventually at eye level with the Manager.

CAPTAIN BROOKS
Where is she?

RETIREMENT HOME MANAGER
This is ridiculous! I can't--

MEL BROOKS
I suggest you give them a hint.

A MOMENT.

MICHELLE
Just tell us!

Captain Thomas twists the Manager's arm a little
more.

RETIREMENT HOME MANAGER
Ok!... Ok! She's at the LA County
Emergency. We took her there last
night.

Captain Brooks and Captain Thomas need a hand up.
Michelle and Mel help them stand and follow the
Captains out of the
office.

>   RETIREMENT HOME MANAGER (CONT'D)
>   You have to pay your bill.

Michelle and Mel stop at the door, looking at the
Manager recouping on the floor.

>   RETIREMENT HOME MANAGER (CONT'D)
>   This is a business...bills need to
>   be paid.

>   MICHELLE
>   You dumped her.

>   MEL BROOKS
>   (to Retirement Manager)
>   You people ought to be ashamed of
>   yourself.

Michelle and Mel leave, closing the door.

DINING ROOM

Michelle and Mel follow the two Captains. They
walk past the Residents at their breakfast. Mr.
and Mrs. Mizrahi still sit at their table; Mrs.
Mizrahi is spoon fed the last of her breakfast
from Mr. Mizrahi. He wipes her chin with his
white handkerchief. Mr. Mizrahi stands and holds
out a hundred-dollar bill, giving it to Captain
Thomas.

>   MR. MIZRAHI
>   It's not much. But tell Lila we
>   love her and we'll do anything to
>   help.

Captain Thomas takes the money. Mrs. Mizrahi
looks up from her plate.

MRS. MIZRAHI
Now Get! Go find our girl.

The Residents lift their knives and forks and
start BANGING on their tables as the two
Captains, Mel and Michelle leave the dining room.
They are clued in with what's going on and
supportive all the way.

EXT. RETIREMENT PLAZA PARKING LOT - MOMENTS LATER

Mel, Michelle and the two Captains head towards
Mel's minivan.

MEL BROOKS
It's a mini van. The only damn
thing I got in the divorce.

MICHELLE
You should see my car.

Mel is in the driver's seat; Michelle is in the
back. The Two Captains stand on the outside of
the car next to the passenger door. Michelle
waits for a MOMENT before looking out to see what
the problem is.

CAPTAIN THOMAS
I always sit in the cockpit.

CAPTAIN BROOKS
I was always at the bridge.

MICHELLE
Come on already.

MEL BROOKS
The only way we'll save Lila is if
one of you takes the backseat.

The Two Captains think about this for a MOMENT.
They get their kids point. Captain Thomas moves
to the back seat door

of the car and gets in. Captain Brooks is already
in the front in his seatbelt.

INT. MEL'S MINI VAN - CONTINUOUS

From the front seat.

          CAPTAIN BROOKS
      (taunting Captain Thomas)
    Look who's the co-pilot now?

From the back seat, the Captain of the air scuffs
the hat of the Captain of the Sea.

          CAPTAIN THOMAS
    We'll see who the deadhead is on
        the way back.

Mel looks in the rearview mirror at Michelle,
they both smile and accept "it is what it is."

    EXT. LOS ANGELES EMERGENCY - LATER

Mel parks the car. The two Captains, Michelle and
Mel jump out and move towards the front entrance.

           MICHELLE
    Let's do this quickly. I got a bank
    manager that can't wait to see me
         late again.

          CAPTAIN THOMAS
    Chuck? He was such a nice guy. Good
      looking boy that one.

Captain Thomas stops, remembering.

      CAPTAIN THOMAS (CONT'D)
    I thought you two were dating?

           MICHELLE
    Were dating. Things changed when I

found out he was still married.

                    CAPTAIN BROOKS
         Alone at sea and a bad marriage can
              to that to any sailor.

                    MEL BROOKS
         Let's mind your own business dad.

                    CAPTAIN THOMAS
         He was awfully kind to your mother
                    and I.

                    CAPTAIN BROOKS
              That says something.

                    MICHELLE
         Aye Aye Captains. No disrespect,
         but can we continue with the duty
                    at hand.

         They enter the Emergency doors.

INT. LOS ANGELES EMERGENCY - CONTINUOUS

The Two Captains, Michelle and Mel search the
waiting area. The seats are crowded with the full
range of non-life threatening emergencies. No
Lila in sight.

They approach the front desk reception. Without
looking up, the Hospital reception passes
Michelle a clipboard with an information sheet.

                    HOSPITAL RECEPTION
         Fill this out, return it here when
         you're done. Have some form of ID
              and proof of health insurance.

                    MICHELLE
         We are looking for a woman by the
                    name of Lila--

                         35

CAPTAIN THOMAS AND CAPTAIN BROOKS
Lila Simmons.

The Hospital Reception types in the name on her computer.

HOSPITAL RECEPTION
Yes...she came in at three this
morning. She's no longer admitted.

MEL BROOKS
And? Where did she go?

HOSPITAL RECEPTION
I'm sorry. And you are relatives?

MICHELLE
No, we are her friends and she was
dumped here last night by the West
LA Retirement Plaza.

HOSPITAL RECEPTION
I'm sorry I can't give out any
information regarding patients if
you are not a relative or the
patient has signed a...

The two Captains start to move in. Preparing for their next self defense tactic of getting information. Mel puts his hands up to stop them.

MEL BROOKS
Captains! Hold your plan of action!

MICHELLE
Now you're talking like these two.

Michelle and Mel move in closer to the Hospital Reception.

MICHELLE (CONT'D)
I suggest you act now and give us a
little information where Lila
Simmons is or you'll be down on

your knees and face planted into
the hospital floor.

MEL BROOKS
And everyone knows how dirty the
hospital floors are.

HAROLD (O.S.)
I saw her.

The two Captains, Michelle and Mel turn to Harold
Sanders (the old guy causing traffic the day
before). Harold has a dried trickle of blood down
his face, elbows and knees have been wrapped with
bandages. Michelle recognizes him.

MICHELLE
You're the gentleman I helped over on
Wilshire and--

Harold taps his right ear, turning so his left
ear is exposed
to Michelle.

MICHELLE (CONT'D)
What happened to you?

Harold mimics with his hands that a car failed to
stop and he was crossing the road again.

HAROLD
It... was my fault. I can't hear a
thing out of my right ear.

HOSPITAL RECEPTION (O.S.)
Sir, your paperwork shows you've
been released. What seems to be the
problem?

MICHELLE
This man was hit a car.

MEL
Maybe he just needs to rest awhile.

HOSPITAL RECEPTION
He cannot rest here. We have no
space, I'll have to call security
if he doesn't leave.

Michelle and the two Captains ignore the Hospital
protocol and turn to Harold for answers.

MICHELLE
(into Harold's Left ear)
Her name is Lila Simmons.

Harold turns his left ear to Michelle and the
Captains. They speak louder now and still mime.
It goes with the territory when people think
someone can't hear well.

CAPTAIN THOMAS
(taking his hands to his
face, miming, kisses his
lips like she is
beautiful)
Beautiful face.

CAPTAIN BROOKS
(imitating walking with a
limp)
Has a cane.
(imitating hour glass
figure with his hands)
But a heck of a figure.

Harold nods "Yes."

MICHELLE
Where?

HAROLD
They took her. (a beat) Where they
take everyone else.

MEL BROOKS
Can you show us?

Harold nods "yes."

The Hospital SECURITY approaches the huddle in front of the reception desk.

                    SECURITY
        What seems to be the problem here?

Harold remembers to grab his bag of belongings of life possessions. The two Captains and Michelle are already on their way out.

                    MICHELLE
        The system. That's our problem.

They leave out the emergency doors.

EXT. LOS ANGELES EMERGENCY - MOMENTS LATER

The two Captains pace quickens as they get closer to Mel's mini van, their competition of first man to the car gets the front seat.

Michelle, Mel and Harold follow behind. Captain Thomas wins the cockpit; Captain Brooks is in the back with the others.

EXT. STREETS OF DOWNTOWN LOS ANGELES - LATER

The mini van drives a busy one-way street of Los Angeles. The daily rush of downtown pushes Mel's mini van along with the traffic. Skyscrapers shade the streets between "mom and pop" stores, the employed and homeless go about their day, sharing the same sidewalk.

INT. MINI VAN - CONTINUOUS

Michelle and Mel are checking in with their work on their cell phones.

                    MICHELLE
                  (into phone)
          Just tell him I'll be in late.
          An emergency came up. Thanks.

                   MEL BROOKS
                  (into phone)
          Put the file on my desk and I'll
          get to it after lunch. Thanks.

They hang up. From the back seat...

                  CAPTAIN BROOKS
          How's it going with your divorce.

                   MEL BROOKS
          Let's find Lila. More important
          than talking about my divorce.

Harold taps Mel on the shoulder from the backseat
telling him to make a right. He stops before
making a right, to let a pedestrian get across.
Horns BLAST wanting him to make a right. Mel
BLASTS his horn back.

                     MEL
          Okay! Okay! What am I supposed do
          do? Run the people over?

                  CAPTAIN BROOKS
                (referring to Harold)
          That's exactly what they did to the
          poor sailor next to me.

Mel makes the right. They drive slowly down a
street.

EXT. STREETS OF DOWNTOWN LOS ANGELES - DAY -
CONTINUOUS

It's a street that appears to be dedicated to
people that live on the streets of Los Angeles.
Plastic tarps provide

shelters, draped over shopping carts. Few sleep, blankets covering their heads.

> CAPTAIN THOMAS (O.S.)
> Oh...sweet Lila. She must be so angry with her family for allowing this to happen to her.

INT. MEL'S MINI VAN - MOMENTS LATER

All eyes glued to their opened windows, searching for Lila.

> CAPTAIN BROOKS
> There she is!

EXT. LOS ANGELES BUS STOP - CONTINUOUS

Lila, we now see that she is AFRICAN AMERICAN, sits under the awning. She has a suitcase next to her. She's waiting for the bus.

Mini van pulls up in front and they all jump out. At the sight of the two Captains, Lila begins to get emotional. The two Captains take their turn to embrace her. She looks up at Michelle and Mel.

> MEL
> What a terrible thing to do to you.

> MICHELLE
> Don't be frightened Lila. I'm so happy we found--

> LILA
> I'm not Fucking frightened! I'm fucking well pissed off! I knew they wanted me out of there. God Damn Mother Fuckers told me I could take a hit of pot last night for the first time in my room, take away a little of this fucking pain

41

I should have known they were up to
something. I'm fucking flying high
and the next thing you know, I wake
up at the Fucking emergency!
Bastards! I should have known they
were Fucking up to something.

Michelle and Mel are speechless. They look at the
two Captains. The two Captains smile with
compassion and move in one more time to embrace
their Lila.

                    CAPTAIN THOMAS
          We are so happy you're okay.

                    CAPTAIN BROOKS
          Had us worried to death.

The two Captains help Lila into the car. (This
time the two Captains get in the back with Lila.)
Michelle and Mel are still stunned by a Lila they
weren't expecting.

                    HAROLD
          You should have heard what she said
                 at the emergency.

Michelle offers the front seat to Harold and
jumps in the back with the others.

INT. MEL'S MINI VAN - MOMENTS LATER

Mel assesses the situation. Looking in his rear
view mirror, he catches Michelle's eye. They
really have no idea what to do next.

                    MEL
          Now where are we going?

                    LILA
          I can't go back to that fucking
             place. They wouldn't have
                  me anyway.

42

                    CAPTAIN THOMAS
        I'm not going back without Lila.

                    CAPTAIN BROOKS
            I'm with you on that one.

Harold pipes up from the front seat.

                        HAROLD
            Can I go stay at the plaza?

Michelle let's out a huge SIGH and an expression
of "what do we do?"

                       MICHELLE
                       (to Mel)
        Could we stop at the bank before we
        go get my car at the plaza? It's on
                      the way.

                    CAPTAIN THOMAS
        Still have that great coffee in the
                    lounge area?

                    CAPTAIN BROOKS
        Great lollipops at some banks.

                      MEL BROOKS
        We can stop. I'm not expected until
                    after lunch.

                       MICHELLE
        I'll make it quick. Should only be
            there for a few minutes.

                        LILA
        It'll give me some time to explain
                    my plan.

Everyone seems fine with that. The mini van is on
its way to the bank.

INT. BANK OF AMERICA - LATER

Michelle enters the bank. Chuck is close to her
desk, speaking with a CUSTOMER. The customer
leaves, Chuck approaches Michelle.

> CHUCK HARRIS
> What's with the entourage?

Michelle looks up to see, the two Captains, Lila
and Harold enter the bank.

> CAPTAIN THOMAS
> Coffee?

Michelle points to the coffee next to a lounge
area. Harold, Lila and Captain Thomas head over
to the coffee. Captain Brooks has found the
basket of lollipops. He helps himself to a few
and takes a few over to the others.

> MICHELLE
> (to Chuck)
> Long story. We'll only be here for
> a few minutes.

Chuck eyes Harold's homeless appearance.

> CHUCK HARRIS
> But the homeless guy. This isn't a
> homeless shelter.

Mel enters the bank talking on his cell phone. He
looks at Michelle and mouths the words "Sorry."
Michelle waves it off that it's okay that the
entourage joined her in her bank lounge. Mel goes
back outside to continue his calls.

> CHUCK HARRIS (CONT'D)
> (referring to Mel)
> Who's he?

> MICHELLE
> You know what, Chuck. I'll be

working from home today, they'll be
out of here in two minutes.

Captain Thomas approaches Chuck and Michelle with
a cup of coffee for himself and a coffee for
Michelle.

> CAPTAIN THOMAS
> Chuck, so good to see you again.

> CHUCK HARRIS
> Oh yes...nice to see you Captain
> Thomas.
> Michelle told me of your wife
> passing six months ago. I'm very
> sorry.

Michelle sits down and tries to get to work, even
with her father and Chuck hanging out in
conversation in front of her desk.

> CAPTAIN THOMAS
> Yes...thank you. She was very sick.
> I forgot that you had met her. She
> liked you, we all had dinner over
> at the little cafe on Main--

> CHUCK HARRIS
> Ah...yes. That's right. Well I
> should be getting back to work.

> CAPTAIN THOMAS
> Michelle tells me you really pulled
> one over on her.

Michelle looks up from her desk.

> MICHELLE
> Dad!

Michelle looks around the bank; it seems a few
are eavesdropping as well as her.

                    CAPTAIN THOMAS
      No... it's ok Michelle. I understand
      how hard it is to be faithful after
      so many years of marriage. I was
        flying all over the world in my
                    pilot days.
                (he's remembering)
      Yes... lots of temptation all over
      the world. Mile high club didn't
      get its name for nothing. Hope it
        all works out for you Chuck.

Chuck doesn't exactly know how to respond.
Thankfully he notices a BANK CUSTOMER waiting for
him at his desk.

                    CHUCK HARRIS
      Well...like I said Captain Thomas.
            Good to see you again.
                (to Michelle)
                Two minutes!

Chuck is already on his way back to his desk.

                    CAPTAIN THOMAS
                (a little salute))
        Keep that fly in check boy.

Chuck stops, looks down, zips up his zipper and
leaves as quickly as he arrived. Captain Thomas
sits down on the chair in front of Michelle's
desk.

                CAPTAIN THOMAS (CONT'D)
          Poor idiot. He loves you.

                      MICHELLE
        Dad...please don't say that.

                    CAPTAIN THOMAS
      But it's the truth. Sometimes you
      stay in marriages because of kids
      and finances. He's a stuck guy. I
        feel sorry for him actually.

                    MICHELLE
        Oh really. Is that how you felt
        when you were married to mom?

                 CAPTAIN THOMAS
        I never stopped loving your mother.
          But I was hardly ever home
        Michelle. I was busy trying to make
        a living before the airline went
        belly up. Then I was busy trying to
        find another job (a beat) and then
               your mother got sick.

                    MICHELLE
        Lila isn't anything like mom. You
          think she's more your type?

                 CAPTAIN THOMAS
        Lila's different. When you get to
          be my age, different is a good
        thing. Everything else is so God
               damn the same.

Michelle looks over at Captain Brooks and Lila in
a serious conversation.

                    MICHELLE
        But dad, to be honest, it seems
        like she's bouncing between you and
               Captain Brooks.

                 CAPTAIN THOMAS
        At my age, a little help with a
        woman like that, isn't such a bad
                    thing.

Michelle takes a MOMENT, digesting her father's
take on life.

                    MICHELLE
        You're telling me the truth about
               loving mom?

CAPTAIN THOMAS
Of course. Truth is all you got at
my age. Your body breaks down, you
hope to God that when death does
get you, it will take you quickly
and painlessly. Old people become a
nuisance. Put us in a retirement
home, if you can afford it, let
someone else take care of us until
we croak. Who wants to change a
diaper? I didn't want to do it with
your mother. It's like having a
child all over again.

MICHELLE
You never changed one diaper when I
was a kid.

CAPTAIN THOMAS
Hell right, I didn't change kids
diapers. But your mother certainly
got me back, didn't she?

MICHELLE
She got you back in more ways then
one.

CAPTAIN THOMAS
Whoever would have thought she'd
lose it all at the blackjack table?

Michelle shakes her head in disbelief.

CAPTAIN THOMAS (CONT'D)
Dementia is a strange beast my
darling.

MICHELLE
She really lost everything at the
gambling table, all in ten minutes?

CAPTAIN THOMAS
I went to the bathroom, came back
and she was surrounded by the police.

MICHELLE
What did you think?

CAPTAIN THOMAS
At that moment, I didn't know what
to think. (a beat) But for forty
years she was the best co-pilot a
man could ever ask for.

MICHELLE
Do you think you were a good
husband?

They both smile sadly, missing the woman in their
lives that meant so much to them.

CAPTAIN THOMAS
In the end. I was a good husband.
(a beat) God rest her sweet soul.
(a beat) What were we talking about
before the blackjack table?

MICHELLE
Truth.

CAPTAIN THOMAS
Right...truth. If you can't speak
your mind, your truth (a beat) then
you've got nothing. Cause
everything else fails you.

Captain Thomas throws his coffee cup in the bin
next to Michelle's desk, starts to walk back to
the others but stops and turns.

CAPTAIN THOMAS (CONT'D)
This last year has been tough on
you. Hang in there. This old guy
will figure it out.

Captain Thomas winks at his daughter and goes
back to the group in the lounge area. Michelle
let's out a deep sigh. The last year has
definitely not been easy.

BANK ENTRANCE

Mel enters the bank, putting away his cell, he walks towards Michelle.

MICHELLE'S DESK

Michelle places the last of her things in her briefcase.

> MICHELLE
> I'm sorry...it's taking me more
> time--

> MEL
> No problem. I got some lawyer calls
> taken care of.

> MICHELLE
> That doesn't sound fun.

> MEL
> Oh she's having the time of her
> life. I'm suppose to be happy she
> gave me the minivan.

Mel's phone rings. He looks at it and turns it off.

> MEL (CONT'D)
> Work will have to wait a moment.

> MICHELLE
> What do you do?

> MEL
> Accountant.

> MICHELLE
> I could do with an accountant to
> show me how to stay on top of it.

> MEL
> Me too.

Michelle looks at him with a little surprise.

> MEL (CONT'D)
> Divorce and a father that had a
> drinking...long story. I'll save
> that one for another time.

> MICHELLE
> Okay. Let's get the Captains back
> to the plaza and you can get to
> work.

Michelle and Mel walk towards two Captains Harold
and Lila, all in deep, hushed conversation in the
lounge area. Lila seems to be at the head of the
discussion.

> LILA
> I'm all out of fucking steam guys,
> I don't feel like there's any other
> way--

> MICHELLE
> What way are we talking about?

SILENCE in the lounge area. Everyone shrugs.
Michelle eyes them all.

> MEL
> Come on you guys, you're in deep
> discussion about something.

SILENCE. More shrugging.

> MICHELLE
> (to Mel)
> I feel like a school teacher
> interrogating a group of school
> kids.

Harold stands.

HAROLD
(to Michelle and Mel)
I just wanted to thank you both for
your kindness. It's been so nice to
have met some new friends. I will
be going now.

MICHELLE
Where?

Harold turns his left ear towards Michelle.

MICHELLE (CONT'D)
Where are you going?

Harold points to the outside, insinuating the
outside is his home.

MEL BROOKS
I'll can take you, Harold.

HAROLD
I'll walk.

MICHELLE
It's too far.

HAROLD
Oh...I'd say nothings too far for
me. The War and 1950 Olympics, they
got me prepared for all of this.
These old legs can still make it a
couple of blocks.

Michelle and Mel look at each other, impressed by
Harold.

MICHELLE
Did you compete in the Olympics?

Harold turns his left ear towards her.

MICHELLE (CONT'D)
What did you compete in?

                    HAROLD
          Ah...Cross country and long jump.

Harold lifts his prayer stick out of his pocket.

                    HAROLD (CONT'D)
          I won a silver with this in my
                    right hand.

Mel takes the prayer stick out of Harold's hand
and admires it.

                    HAROLD (CONT'D)
          It has been with me since I was a
                    child

Harold smiles a toothless smile, finding the
humor in this. Harold hugs Lila, salutes the
Captains and slowly goes down onto one knee, as
if getting ready to start a race.

Lila lifts her right hand, pretending she's the
starter of a race.

                    LILA
          On your mark runners.
          (a beat) Set (a beat) BANG!

Harold doesn't move, Lila is on his right side.
               Lila moves to
            Harold's left side.

                    LILA (CONT'D)
          (into Harold's left ear)
                    BANG!

Harold sprints (as much as a man can that's in
his 90's) to the front doors of the bank and
turns around as everyone CLAPS for his victory
win. He smiles and leaves.

Their smiles turn to compassion as they watch a
sweet man go back to the streets.

> MEL BROOKS
> Our country needs to figure out a
> better plan for people like Harold.

Chuck interrupts them.

> CHUCK HARRIS
> What was that bizarre thing that
> just happened?

> MICHELLE
> (to herself)
> An attitude adjustment, that's what
> America needs. See you tomorrow
> Chuck.

> MEL BROOKS
> Let's go crew.

The two Captains, Lila and Michelle follow Mel
out the doors.

INT. MEL'S MINI VAN - MOMENTS LATER

Again, the two Captains sit in the back with Lila
in the middle. Michelle is in the front.

> LILA
> Take me to one hundred, Green
> street. Santa Monica, North of
> Montana.

Mel looks at Michelle next to her in the
passenger seat.

> MEL
> Why is it that I'm feeling like a
> taxi driver?

Michelle and Mel turn and look at Lila. She
motions them to drive ahead.

EXT. 100 GREEN STREET - LATER

Mini van pulls over on the street. A small, older house builtin the 1950's sits between two multi-million-dollar modern homes. It's maintained but an eyesore for the rest of the wealthy neighbors. A FOR SALE sign is posted on the front lawn with large letters SOLD across it.

EXT. MEL'S MINI VAN - CONTINUOUS

The two Captains and Lila get out of the car. Michelle looks out the passenger window.

The two Captains hug Lila good-bye.

                    MICHELLE
          Your family lives here?

                    LILA
               A friend.

                    MEL
          You're going to be okay?

                    LILA
          It will work out.

The two Captains hug Lila.

                    LILA (CONT'D)
          You remember everything.

The two Captains nod "yes. "Lila takes her bag in one hand and cane in the other, she walks towards the front door of the home.

                    LILA (CONT'D)
          See you soon.

                         MICHELLE
                         (confused)
            Ah...yes...see you soon.

The two Captains jump in the back.

                           MEL
            What was that all about?

Michelle and Mel turn around eyeing their
fathers.

                      MEL (CONT'D)
                         Dad?

Captain Brooks shrugs, he's not telling.

                         MICHELLE
                         Dad?

Captain Thomas shrugs, he's not telling either.

                     MICHELLE (CONT'D)
                  (demanding an answer)
            Okay...what's going on?

            SILENCE... more shrugging.

      Mel looks in his rear view mirror at the
                Captains, something
            is definitely up between them.

                           MEL
            I gotta get to work.

Michelle looks at Mel. It's been a long day for
both of themand they are not in the mood to
interrogate.

EXT. MICHELLE'S APARTMENT - MORNING

Michelle is just coming back from her morning
run. Walking up the stairs, she notices that not

only her plants are coming back to life and
watered but a few empty planters have
additional flowers planted. Michelle smiles and
goes inside.

INT. MICHELLE'S APARTMENT - CONTINUOUS

Michelle does her usual message check.

CLOSE-UP CELL PHONE DISPLAYS NO MESSAGES.

Michelle goes straight to her home answering
machine and presses the button for messages.

                    ANSWERING MACHINE
                 (computerized voice)
              You have no messages.

Michelle picks up her phone and starts to dial.
She puts it down.

                    MICHELLE
                 (to herself)
              He's a big boy. He's okay.

No emergency message from Captain Thomas not only
confuses her but leaves her plenty of time to
actually walk to the shower and not run.

INT. BANK OF AMERICA - LATER

Michelle enters the bank. This time EVERYONE
looks up upon her arrival, not because she's late
but because she's early.
Michelle has time this morning to get herself a
coffee.

Chuck has already poured her a cup and hands it
to her.

                    CHUCK HARRIS
              Two sugars, little cream just the
                 way you like it.

Michelle takes it from him and heads to her desk.

                    MICHELLE
                    Thanks.

Chuck follows her and stands in front of her desk
as she sits down to get to work.

                    CHUCK HARRIS
            I think we need to talk.

Michelle looks up from her desk.

                    MICHELLE
        Something's wrong with my dad. He
        didn't call me with an emergency
                this morning.

                    CHUCK HARRIS
            That's a good thing, isn't it?

                    MICHELLE
            But it's normal for him to call
                with an emergency.

Chuck looks over to the entrance of the bank.

                    CHUCK HARRIS
            Are you going to be bringing these
            people to work with you everyday
                        now?

Michelle looks up, Mel has entered the bank and
is headed straight for her.

                    MEL
            Good morning. I didn't have your
            number to call but... I think we
                have a bit of a problem.

                    MICHELLE
                What's wrong?

                    MEL
     Ah... it's concerning the Captains.
      I think there's a potential
     problem... their up to something, I
           have no idea what but--

                 CHUCK HARRIS
        Your problem will have to wait
        until later. Looks like the First
        Lady and Hilary have just paid us a
                    visit.

Michelle and Mel look towards the door.

TWO BANK ROBBERS have entered the bank with the
security guard at gun point. He drops his gun and
lies down on the floor. Dressed in flowered
dresses, wigs, flowered brimmed hats, white
gloves and a mask of HILARY CLINTON and the FIRST
LADY, (MICHELLE OBAMA) is their crazy disguise.
Hilary Clinton waves her gun at the TELLERS and
FEW CUSTOMERS, hands now above their heads, they
move to the open floor.

                 HILARY CLINTON
                 Move it folks!

The First Lady has her gun pointed at Michelle,
Mel and Chuck, hands above their heads.

                   FIRST LADY
        Everyone down on the ground. Face
                    down!

Everyone gets down on their knees and begin to
lie down on the floor.

The First Lady throws a floral large purse to
Michelle.

              FIRST LADY (CONT'D)
              You! Fill it. Go!

Michelle takes the purse and runs behind the teller counter. She fills the purse with stacks of bills.

CLOSE-UP OF MICHELLE'S FOOT PRESSING DOWN THE EMERGENCY BUTTON ON THE FLOOR.

Michelle returns with the purse of money. It's full and it's wide open, full of bills. She places the purse at feet of the First Lady.

> MICHELLE
> You think the President would
> approve of this?

> FIRST LADY
> Funny.

Mel peeks up from the floor.

> MEL
> I always wanted to meet you two.
> Never thought it would be like
> this.

> HILARY CLINTON
> Neither did I.

The First Lady points her gun at Michelle, waving it at her to get the basket of lollipops off the deposit counter.

CLOSE-UP OF "Toy's r Us" price tag hanging from the gun.

The First Lady angles herself so the price tag cannot be seen by Michelle.

> FIRST LADY
> All of them... inside.

Michelle looks at the full purse. There's no room for the lollipops.

> MICHELLE
> How? Ah... there's no room.

The First Lady quickly takes out enough money, dropping it on the floor, allowing room for the lollipops. The First Lady takes two lollipops and then waves her gun at Michelle to pour the lollipops inside the purse and close it.

> FIRST LADY
> Thanks. Please lie down.

Michelle gets down on the ground face first, like the others.

> HILARY CLINTON
> Let's go... time's running out.

(O.S.) SIRENS are heard in close distance.

The First Lady grabs the flowered purse and heads to the front door with Hilary Clinton.

AT THE BANK DOOR

The First Lady and Hilary quickly whip off their wig and mask and let them fall to the floor. Delia Zamora (the Spanish woman that had the problem with the ATM) was Hilary Clinton and the First Lady is now Lila Simmons.

They exit the bank.

EXT. BANK OF AMERICA - MORNING

Delia and Lila quickly scan each other over. Their new attire of flowered dresses and flowered brim hats make them look like retired citizens just out to make their morning bank deposit.

> DELIA ZAMORA
> You sure this plan will work?

Lila opens up the two lollipops and passes one to Delia.

                    LILA
          Lick it and feel your age.

The first Police car to the scene screeches up in front of the bank. Two POLICEMEN jump out, rifles in hand. POLICEMAN #1 runs around the side entrance of the bank.

                    POLICE 1
          Get the grannies out of the way!

POLICEMAN #2 grabs Lila and Delia and pushes them off to safety.

                    POLICE 2
          Keep walking ladies. We have a
                robbery going on.

Lila and Delia both look at him sweetly.

                    LILA
          What a lovely man. Thank you.

                    DELIA
          Serve and protect.

Delia and Lila walk away from the scene of the crime as ten more LAPD Police cars show up on the scene.

                    LILA
          Our getaway car is right on time.

The city bus has just arrived at the bus stop next to the bank.

Delia and Lila get on the bus.

INT. CITY BUS - CONTINUOUS

Lila and Delia move towards one empty seat at the back of the crowded bus. Lila shifts in her feet, she doesn't have her cane to lean on today.

                    LILA
          I need my cane.

              DELIA ZAMORA
      Your hip is bothering you. Sit
                 down.

Lila seldom likes to admit she's in pain but decides to take the seat next to a JOSEPH GUERRERO (20's) with earphones in his ears. He looks at Delia standing above him and then to Lila sitting next to him. His expression conveys he recognizes them. Joseph stands and offers his seat to Delia.

           DELIA ZAMORA (CONT'D)
              Gracias.

Delia takes the seat by the window. Lila has the flowered purse on her lap and places it at her feet. In hushed voices.

                    LILA
      I don't remember having so much
      fucking fun since the time I stood
      up and cursed out the entire LA
              School board.

Delia and Lila get the GIGGLES.

               LILA (CONT'D)
      I mean... fucking seriously, did
      you see the way Chuck the Shmuck
      looked at us when we walked in
                 there?

              DELIA ZAMORA
          Did you see my gun?

Lila shakes her head "No."

DELIA ZAMORA (CONT'D)
I forgot to take the "Toys r Us"
price tag off. I thought for sure
Michelle saw the Toys'R'Us price
tag.

LILA
Remind me to never rob a bank with
an amateur again.

Their GIGGLES turn to a more serious tone.

LILA (CONT'D)
(looking out the window))
Yep... Never thought my fucking
life would come to this.

DELIA ZAMORA
You're a champ Lila. You stood up
for me in that boardroom... I can't
ever repay you enough.

LILA
They framed you of stealing that
kids lunch money. Fucking bastards.
They knew you didn't steal it.

DELIA ZAMORA
Yes... but... they wanted me out. I
lied on my resume. I should have
known they'd find out sooner or
later.

LILA
You were a damned fucking good...
honest janitor. And don't you
forget it! That school was the
cleanest and most organized I had
ever seen it and every kid... and
every parent loved you. I should
know, I saw many janitors pass
through that school. You did your
job better than anyone else, so
what if your past involved a crime

and you had to serve a little time.
You were just trying to survive.

                    DELIA ZAMORA
No... not you. You were the perfect
Principle. You believed in everyone
and I saw how every kid got a
chance at that school. (a beat) The
school board knew that.

                    LILA
They were happy to see me go. I
wasn't one to listen to their
bullshit. Fuckers. (a moment)
I miss them. (a beat) The kids...
some of the parents. If they could
see me now?

A MOMENT between them. They glance at Joseph,
he's removed one of his earphones and has been
listening to their conversation. He quickly puts
his earphones back in.

Lila looks at her watch.

                    LILA (CONT'D)
I hope our lunch is ready.

                    DELIA
What did you order.

                    LILA
Some good old fashion American
hamburgers, greasy fries and the
classic vanilla shake.

                    DELIA ZAMORA
Sounds like the perfect last meal
to me.

EXT. SANTA MONICA STREETS/ TOP HAT HAMBURGERS -
LATER
The bus pulls up at a bus stop in front of a "mom
and pop" hamburger shack.

INT. CITY BUS - CONTINUOUS

Lila gets up slowly, a grimace on her face, her
hips bugging her.

                    DELIA
          That's the first thing you get
            taken care of when we go in.

Delia and Lila follow a few PASSENGERS off the
bus.

                    JOSEPH
          Senorita... I think you forgot your
                      bag.

Delia and Lila turn. Lila takes the flowered bag
from Joseph.

                JOSEPH (CONT'D)
              Do I know you?

Delia and Lila look at each other, knowing smile.

                    LILA
          You're one of the Guerrero family.

                    JOSEPH
              Ah... yes... Joseph.

                    DELIA
          You were the youngest of three
                    brothers.

                    JOSEPH
                  (to Lila)
            Yeah!... Yeah! That's it!
            You were that cool principle.
                  (to Delia)
          And... you were... you worked as
                the janitor at--

                    LILA
            She kept you boys in line.

Joseph is speechless, he remembers these women
fondly.

                    BUS DRIVER (O.S.)
          Can't wait all day. Let's go folks!

                         LILA
                  Your mother's well?

                        JOSEPH
          Yeah... My brother's and I try and
          help her out... she's getting older-

Lila quietly slips a stack of money into Joseph's
hand.

                         LILA
          She was a single mother and raised
             three good boys. Tell her I say
                        hello.

Lila and Delia leave the bus. Joseph finds a seat
next to the window and looks out as the bus pulls
away.

EXT. TOP HAT HAMBURGERS - CONTINUOUS

Delia and Lila step off the bus. A taxi driver
pulls up almost immediately.

                         LILA
          We should have thought about doing
                  this for a living.

TAXI DRIVER yells out his window.

                      TAXI DRIVER
          You two ladies ordered a cab?

Delia walks to the taxi cab driver's window.

                    DELIA
        Right on time. Pull around back.
        We'll be out in a few minutes.

The taxi cab drives around back, Delia and Lila
open the door and go inside the hamburger shack.

INT. BANK OF AMERICA - A FEW HOURS LATER

Michelle and Chuck stand by the lounge area. Mel
is pacing on his cell phone. The Investigation of
the bank robbery is underway as the other
Employees are questioned by
INVESTIGATORS.

                    MICHELLE
        No one saw them get away?

                    CHUCK HARRIS
        Apparently the first cop on the
        scene helped them escape. Thought
        they were two old grandmas out for
                a morning walk.

                    MICHELLE
        Wow... he'll probably never live
                that one down.

                    CHUCK HARRIS
        They'll find them. Everything in
        the area has been locked down.

                    MICHELLE
        Maybe they jumped on a city bus?

                    CHUCK HARRIS
        Grannies don't jump. (a beat) But
        good point. They're checking the
        surveillance cameras now to see if
                they can identify them.

Chuck walks to the corner where INVESTIGATORS, POLICE AND PERSONAL hover over surveillance footage.

INT. CITY BUS - LATER

Joseph sits on the bus with other PASSENGERS. He lifts out his wad of bills, eyes them and then slips them back into his pocket. He looks out the window.

Sounds of police SIRENS approach. Joseph can't help but smile.

INT. BANK OF AMERICA

Mel is still pacing with his cell phone to his ear. Michelle is listening to his conversation.

> MEL
> (into cell)
> Ok... let me know if there is any
> change. Yes... call me on this
> number. Thank you.

Mel puts his phone away. They move in closer to speak.

> MICHELLE
> What did you mean the bus didn't
> show up at the museum?

> MEL
> That's what I was trying to tell
> you before the robbery. On my way
> to work, I was dropping off a few
> more things of my dad's at the
> plaza and the receptionist told me
> that the bus going on the field
> trip to the museum left before the
> activity supervisor could get on
> the bus.

>   MICHELLE
>   Left without the supervisor. (a
>   beat) My dad hates field trips.

>   MEL
>   Mine never went on a field trip in
>   his life.

>   MICHELLE
>   So what do you think is going on?

>   MEL
>   Twenty old folks, a bus and a
>   driver have vanished.

>   MICHELLE
>   The Captains were acting bizarre
>   yesterday--

>   MEL
>   As soon as we can get out of here,
>   we'll head over there.

INT. 100 GREEN STREET - LIVING ROOM - AFTERNOON -
SAME TIME

Lila stands at the front of what looks to be a
seminar in full swing. She holds a milkshake in
one hand, sipping from the straw, at the same
time she's in lecture mode.

Delia sits next to her, enjoying a burger while
listening to the lecture. Lila writes on one
large chalkboard.

CLOSE-UP OF CHALKBOARD showing a schematic titled
"CRIME AND PUNISHMENT. Under the title are two
columns, one is FEDERAL PRISON and one is STATE
PRISON. Carjacking, marry a spouse of another,
sale of human organs, money laundering, seduction
of minors for prostitution, already have a line
through them. Lila has been listing them off.

Pimping, manslaughter, Robbery-first degree, Robbery-second degree are the last to discuss.

Lila looks at her watch, turns back to the wall and precedes to go through the last few crimes on the list.

> LILA
> Pimping. If any of you really think
> you have what it takes to run a sex
> ring, then why didn't you tell me
> before I went and robbed a bank.

A few CHUCKLES, Lila crosses off the word "pimping." She crosses out the word manslaughter a few times.

> LILA (CONT'D)
> No one gets hurt. That's why
> robbery is our best way to go.

Lila circles "Robbery-first degree, Robbery-second degree."

> LILA (CONT'D)
> Real guns are out. You'll be
> supplied with the top of the line
> plastic weapons. Any questions?

PULL OUT TO REVEAL AUDIENCE

Captain Thomas and Captain Buckley pace at the back of the room. The house appears to be vacant, only a few old chairs.

TEN RETIREMENT PENSIONERS from the plaza sit in a few of the chairs, a few in wheelchairs, some stand on the side with their walkers. They are all finishing up their feast of burgers, fries and milkshakes, listening to this informative seminar.

A MUFFLED VOICE is heard from the corner of the room.

Everyone looks over to RICK KENT (60's) He sits on a chair, his hands are tied and his mouth is gagged.

> CAPTAIN BROOKS
> He's been trying to speak for the last hour, can we give him a few words?

Everyone nods "yes."

Captain Thomas takes Rick Kent's gag off.

> RICK KENT
> Hi... my name is Rick.

> EVERYONE
> Hello Rick.

> RICK KENT
> Can I... join?

Everyone takes a MOMENT. The consensus of the room is "yes."
Captain Thomas and Captain Brooks untie him.

KNOCK at the door interrupts the seminar.

Captain Brooks and Captain Thomas are immediately at the door, Lila hushes everyone QUIET.

> HAROLD (O.S.)
> It's me... Harold

> CAPTAIN BROOKS
> Who goes there?

The Captains look at each other, not trusting what's on the other side of the door.

> CAPTAIN THOMAS
> Boarding pass?

At the front of the room, Lila writes on the
chalkboard, "It's a beautiful day @ the plaza."

> HAROLD (O.S.)
> It's a beautiful day at the...
> plaza?

Audience nods in agreement.

Lila gives the Captains the go ahead to unlock
the door.

Harold enters quickly.

> HAROLD (CONT'D)
> Sorry I'm late. It... was a long
> walk.

The two Captains shake Harold's hand.

> LILA
> Harold, the others can fill you in.
> (a beat) Captain Thomas and Captain
> Brooks will take it from here and
> answer everyone's questions at a
> later time.

> DELIA
> We gotta get them out of here.
> Clock's ticking.

> LILA
> I will miss you all. You have
> become family. I'll see some of you
> again soon. Gather your things and
> leave by the back door.

> DELIA
> Let's move everyone.

The entire room gathers their belongings and
begin to move slowly, some with walkers, canes
and few help the others in wheelchairs. They
leave the room through the back door.

INT. BANK OF AMERICA.

JOHN DOE, CHIEF INVESTIGATOR OF THE LA DEPARTMENT
OF JUSTICE approaches Michelle and Mel.

          JOHN DOE
      Come take a look.

Michelle and Mel quickly follow John towards the
back of the room.

They join Chuck, a few police, security guard and
few employees in front of a computer screen.

CLOSE-UP OF VIDEO FOOTAGE - Delia and Lila stand
at the front of the bank, they take their masks
off.

          MICHELLE
        Lila?

        SGT. JOHN DOE
     Do you know this woman?

          MEL
     That's Lila... Simmons.

        SGT. JOHN DOE
   Who is Lila Simmons. Which one is
         she?

         MICHELLE
     (looking at footage)
   And that's Mrs... what's her
name?... The Spanish woman that was
    in our bank the day before.

       CHUCK HARRIS
  And both of you know Lila! She's
  your friend. What are you guys not
      telling us?

         MICHELLE
Lila is not my friend, she lives in

the same retirement home as my dad.

                    SGT. JOHN DOE
        Do you have Lila Simmons address?

                    MICHELLE
        Yes... it's 801 Ocean Ave. But she
        won't be there because they kicked
                her out yesterday.

Sgt. John Doe is trying to follow all of this.

                    MEL
        Lila was dumped at the emergency.
        We picked her up yesterday morning.

                    SGT. JOHN DOE
        And where did you take her?

                MICHELLE AND MEL
                    Here!

Sgt. John Doe's eyes open a little wider. A
MOMENT.

                    SGT. JOHN DOE
        You brought the suspect here? Ok...
            Do you know Lila Simmons
                    accomplice?

                    MICHELLE
                (trying to remember))
        Yes... she was in here a few days
        ago... I thought I was helping her
                    out.

                    CHUCK HARRIS
                (under his breath)
            Yeah... no kidding.

                    MEL
        Wait! We took Lila to Green street
                after bank.

                    MICHELLE
          Her name is... Delia... Delia
          Zamora.

Sgt. John Doe is already on his phone.

Michelle has moved to a computer and enters the
name of Delia Zamora.

CLOSE UP OF SCREEN - Delia Zamora 100 Green
Street Venice CA 90291.

                 MICHELLE (CONT'D)
          100 Green street. Venice.

Sgt. John Doe is already on the move, into his
radio.

                  SGT. JOHN DOE
          We got an address. 100 Green
                Street. Let's go!

LAPD by his side, Sgt. John Doe turns to
Michelle, Mel and Chuck.

                  SGT.JOHN DOE
          You guys stay put. I have a few
             more questions for you.
            (to LAPD Officer by his
                    side)
          Stay with them. I'll be back.

LAPD Officer stays behind with Chuck, Michelle
and Mel and the FORENSIC EVIDENCE TEAM busy doing
their work.

                  CHUCK HARRIS
                   (to Mel)
             Are you in on this?

Mel blows this question off like it's absurd.
Chuck turns to Michelle.

                    CHUCK HARRIS (CONT'D)
                      (to Michelle)
            And you? What about your dad?

                        MICHELLE
                    Fuck off Chuck!

Chuck looks at them with a smirk, he's not
believing it.

EXT. 100 GREEN STREET - BACKYARD - LATER

Lila stands with Delia, the two Captains and
Harold next to the THE WEST LA RETIREMENT PLAZA
BUS. It has pulled up in the driveway next to the
house and everyone else is inside ready to go.

                          LILA
                      (to Harold)
            Did you get yourself a milkshake?

Harold lifts his milkshake and takeout bag of a
                    hamburger and
                        fries.

                     LILA (CONT'D)
            You'll be able to get some rest
                        soon.

                        HAROLD
            Thank you for including me. God
            knows I'm looking forward to a
                        pillow.

Harold hugs Lila goodbye and begins to walk down
the driveway. He turns and waves.

                    HAROLD (CONT'D)
                   (to the Captains)
            I'll see you tomorrow.

                    CAPTAIN BROOKS
                 Nine-thirty sharp.

The all wave good-bye, as Harold walks out into
the neighborhood.

Captain Thomas followed by Captain Brooks hug
Delia.

> CAPTAIN THOMAS
> It was a pleasure to meet you.

> CAPTAIN BROOKS
> You are one fine woman.

> Delia smiles.

> CAPTAIN THOMAS
> And see to it, our Lila gets her
> hip taken care of.

> DELIA
> On the top of the list.

The Captains turn to Lila and both lift her right
and left hand simultaneously, tears in their
eyes.

> CAPTAIN BROOKS
> (kissing her right hand)
> You were the wind in my sails.

> CAPTAIN THOMAS
> (kissing her left hand)
> And the wind beneath my wings.

They hold her hands one MOMENT longer, they don't
want to let her go.

> LILA
> (loving them)
> You old saps! You make me crazy!
> (shooing them off)
> Now get! Don't mess up the plan!

The Two Captains smile before jumping on the bus as Rick closes the door and backs the bus out into the street. The Bus leaves.

Lila and Delia watch it disappear. After a MOMENT. Lila notices Delia looking up at the house and then to the sign on the front lawn.

> DELIA
> My parents worked so hard for this
> place.

Delia walks over to a fruit tree in the yard and picks an orange off the tree.

Delia walks back to Lila, smelling the orange.

> DELIA (CONT'D)
> I was six when my brother and I
> planted this for my mother's
> birthday. It took ten years until
> we got our first piece of fruit. (a
> beat) My mother cut it into four
> pieces... one for each of us. It
> was the best we had ever tasted. We
> were such a proud... happy...
> Mexican American family.

After a MOMENT. Lila looks over at the FOR SALE/SOLD sign.

> LILA
> Your brother wouldn't have wanted
> them to sell this?

> DELIA
> But he's gone and his kids knew
> they could get a fortune for this
> place.

> LILA
> It's a shame.

                         DELIA
          They left me out of the will and I
          can't blame him. My brother loved
           me, but he never forgave me for
                 hurting my parents.

                          LILA
           Come on, they'll be here soon. We
            need to get our stuff together,
                    let's go inside.

Lila limps with her cane, Delia takes her other
arm and helps her up the few steps leading to the
door. They go inside.

EXT. 100 GREEN STREET - MOMENTS LATER

LAPD and NEWS helicopters circle overhead.

The LAPD cruisers screech to a stop at the front
of the house and move into action. News vans
immediately begin to set up live coverage
cameras. Neighbors appear out of their houses,
creating a commotion in the streets. It's the
scene we see on every cop reality show.

SGT. John Doe immediately arrives in his car and
jumps out.

The LAPD COMMANDER is on the loud speaker.

                    LAPD COMMANDER
            We have you surrounded. Come out
                  with your hands up.

JAKE (5) AND DANIEL OWENS (7), neighborhood boys,
emerge from out of the bushes next to the house,
wide eyed and hands held high in the air. They
hold the two plastic guns that Delia and Lila
used for the robbery.

Everyone's attention is turned to the young boys.

> LAPD COMMANDER (CONT'D)
> Drop your weapons!

The two boys drop their weapons.

> DANIEL
> The... grandmas gave them to us!

> JAKE
> We... didn't steal them. Honest!

LAPD 1 grabs the guns off the ground and LAPD 2 moves the boys away from the line of fire.

LAPD 1 shows the plastic guns to Sgt. John Doe and the LAPD Captain.

> SGT. JOHN DOE
> (admiring the sales tag)
> Toys'R'Us sell a good looking
> handgun.

They look up to the front of the house.

> OVER THE RADIO (O.S.)
> Back door is ready.

> LAPD CAPTAIN
> Let's do this. We're going in.

Sgt. John Doe retrieves his gun out of his chest holster and begins to follow the other LAPD up the front walkway, low and cautiously.

INT. 100 GREEN STREET - CONTINUOUS

The front door SLAMS OPEN. POLICEMAN 3 and 4 enter first, followed by a full team of armored POLICEMEN. Weapons aimed, intensity at its highest.

> POLICEMAN 3
> GET DOWN NOW! DOWN ON YOUR KNEES!

                    POLICEMAN 4
                GET DOWN! GET DOWN!

SILENCE.

Sgt. John Doe moves inside, followed by POLICEMAN
1. Guns aimed to the front of an empty room.

Lila and Delia sit on two chairs, next to the
wall that has the seminar written across it.
They've peeled the orange, their hands held high
in the air still holding on to the last of their
orange treat.

                    SGT. JOHN DOE
            Ladies. Get down on the ground.

Delia tries to get down, but she still has the
last of her orange to eat. Putting it quickly
into her mouth, CLICK! The weapons are raised and
aimed once again. Delia shows her hands, they are
empty now, and she's going to the ground.

Lila tries to move but her hip seems to be locked
as she tries to stand.

                        LILA
                  (to Policeman 1)
            Sonny, could you hand me my cane?

Policeman 1 looks at Sgt. John Doe. He nods his
head "yes."

Policeman 1 grabs Lila's cane that has fallen
just out of Lila's reach and gives it to her. He
looks back at Sgt. John Doe as if asking
permission to help her further. Sgt. John Doe
gives him the go ahead.

Policeman 1 gives Lila her cane and helps her get
to the floor.

                    LILA (CONT'D)
                    Thank you.

                    SGT. JOHN DOE
                    (into radio)
          We have the suspects in custody.
          Two females in their...? My
             Grandmother's age...

Lila looks up from the floor.

                       LILA
                    Eighty-two.

                      DELIA
              Eighty-four next week.

                    SGT. JOHN DOE
                    Thank you.
                    (into radio)
          One black, one Latino. I thought
                I'd seen it all.

INT. WEST LOS ANGELES RETIREMENT PLAZA - LATER

The Retirement Receptionist is on the phone, she
looks up to Michelle and Mel walking through the
door.

             RETIREMENT HOME RECEPTIONIST
                    (into phone)
                May I put you on hold?
                (to Michelle and Mel)
           The bus got back two hours ago.

Michelle and Mel let out a huge SIGH of relief.

                       MEL
                  Are they okay?

             RETIREMENT HOME RECEPTIONIST
           Did you hear about the robbery? It
                was all over the news.

Michelle and Mel look at each other.

                    MEL AND MICHELLE
            Oh yes... we heard about the
                    robbery.

They sign in quickly.

                RETIREMENT HOME MANAGER
            You'll find them all in the game
                    room.

Michelle and Mel walk quickly through the dining
room. Mr. Mizrahi sits alone at his table. A
NURSE drapes a sweater over Mr. Mizrahi's
shoulders and meets Michelle and Mel before they
get to his table.

                    MICHELLE
            Where's Mrs. Mizrahi?

The Nurse's face shows the sad news to Michelle
and Mel.

                    NURSE
            Last night. It was a stroke.

                    MEL
            Does he have family?

                    NURSE
            They're arriving from New York this
            afternoon. (a beat) The police were
            here, questioning everyone that was
            on the bus. Just thought you should
                    know.

                MICHELLE AND MEL
                    Thanks.

The Nurse leaves, Michelle and Mel approach the
table. Michelle sits across the table from Mr.
Mizrahi.

A MOMENT before he wipes his tear stained eyes
with the white handkerchief.

                    MR. MIZRAHI
              (lifting handkerchief)
      She made them out of her wedding
      dress when the doctors told us she
      had dementia. She made me promise
          I'd keep her dignified.

                    MICHELLE
            I'm so sorry Mr. Mizrahi.

                    MR. MIZRAHI
         I hadn't seen her giggle like a
      school girl and have so much fun in years.

Michelle looks up at Mel. They're not following
him at all.

                    MICHELLE
          I'm sorry... I don't know what
                you're talking--

                    MR. MIZRAHI
         A few nights ago, Lila came into
      our room and told us she was going
       to rob a bank and she needed two
         pretty dresses. They gave me a
        private fashion show... in my own
           bedroom. (a beat) Lila was the
        life of the party in this place.

Michelle and Mel smile tenderly and embrace Mr.
Mizrahi.

                    MICHELLE
         Can we do anything for you?

Mr. Mizrahi smiles and shakes his head "no."

                    MR. MIZRAHI
           Everyone's in the lounge.

Michelle and Mel leave towards the activity
lounge.

ACTIVITY LOUNGE

The two Captains sit at a long table with the other RESIDENTS from the retirement plaza bus. A card game is underway but the attention of the players is focused on a wide screen televising the bank robbery and the capture of fugitives Lila Simmons and Delia Zamora.

Michelle and Mel approach the table, eyes on the screen.

TV SCREEN/ LIVE NEWS FOOTAGE

A NEWS REPORTER stands in front of 100 Green Street. Sgt. John Doe is in an interview.

>   REPORTER
>   (on TV)
>   What do you think the motives are
>   behind two elderly women committing
>   such a crime?

>   SGT. JOHN DOE
>   (On TV)
>   I'm not in any position to answer
>   that question but... I can assure
>   you, the suspects have been very
>   cooperative. I think this is a very
>   unusual bank robbery.

RETIREMENT PLAZA/ACTIVITIES LOUNGE

The two Captains stand and meet Michelle and Mel.

>   MEL
>   Start explaining you two.

Captain Thomas and Captain Brooks look at each other and then back to their kids with a dumbfounded shrug.

>   MICHELLE
>   The cops think we are in on this?

CAPTAIN THOMAS
We know that's not true.

MICHELLE
Start telling us the truth
Captains.

CAPTAIN THOMAS
Lila was full of surprises?

CAPTAIN BROOKS
Is she ever.

MICHELLE
Where did you guys go today?

MEL
What happened to the bus, dad?

CAPTAIN BROOKS
Oh... that. Terrible. Our driver
had a blood sugar low--

CAPTAIN THOMAS
Forgot where we were going. Drove
us all the way to Palm Springs.
Poor guy--

CAPTAIN BROOKS
Glad we got his insulin figured
out.

MEL
And the cops believed this story?

CAPTAIN THOMAS
Affirmative. Some trip that was. It
was like spending the entire day on
a runway.

MICHELLE
That's the truth, the whole truth
and nothing but the truth--?

CAPTAIN THOMAS
Stop! He had nothing to do with any
of this.

Michelle and Mel look over at the table of the
Elderly Residents. They've been listening and
they all nod their heads "yes." All in agreement
on this story.

MEL
And Dad, you're sure you knew
nothing about this?

Once again, the two Captains shrug and shake
their head "No."
Everyone else at the table joins in with the
shrugs.

MICHELLE
You realize... it's over for Lila
and her friend Delia. They're going
to have to spend the rest of their
lives in prison.

The two Captains nod their heads "yes."

CAPTAIN BROOKS
Devastating.

CAPTAIN THOMAS
Absolutely mind boggling.

After a MOMENT.

MICHELLE
Well... I'm going home. It's been a
long day. I'm... glad your okay.

MEL
Stay out of trouble. You're up to
something and whatever it is... Be
smart!

CAPTAIN BROOKS
Exactly what I told you when you
were a little boy. At least I
taught you something right.

Michelle and Mel hug their parents and begin to
leave together. Michelle stops and turns, she has
one more question for the Captains.

MICHELLE
If you both cared for her so much,
you must have some idea why she
chose to do this?

CAPTAIN THOMAS
Lila was a proud woman.

MICHELLE
What does that got to do with any
of this?

CAPTAIN BROOKS
When you're our age, you'll
understand.

MEL
Understand what?

CAPTAIN THOMAS
Dead tired tonight.

CAPTAIN BROOKS
Let's call it a day.

Waiting until their kids are out of sight,
Captain Thomas lifts a piece of paper out of his
pocket and stands at the head of the table.
Captain Brooks returns to the opposite head of
the table.

CAPTAIN THOMAS
Tomorrow's field trip. First stop.
Toys R Us.

                    CAPTAIN BROOKS
            Second stop, will be a costume
                        shop.

SARA STANLEY (80's) taps her left ear.

                     SARA STANLEY
            What's he saying? My hearing aid is
                      off again?

CLIVE MARSHALL (70's) sits in a wheel chair next
to her.

                    CLIVE MARSHALL
              Second stop. Costume shop!

                     SARA STANLEY
            Ohhh.... May I make a suggestion?
            Party City Costumes is fantastic! I
               took my grandson years ago.

Captain Thomas and Captain Brooks become very
serious.

                    CAPTAIN THOMAS
            I want to make sure you've all
                thought about this.

                    CAPTAIN BROOKS
            This is a dangerous mission.

                    CAPTAIN THOMAS
            Once in the air, you are past the
            point of no return. This is a one
               way away ticket folks. Any
                      questions?

Everyone shakes their heads "No."

                    CAPTAIN BROOKS
            Captain Thomas is right. You have
            time to reconsider until tomorrow.
            I suggest you return to your cabins
               early this evening, get a good

night's sleep and eat a good
breakfast before departure.
The bus leaves port at precisely 09
hundred.

Everyone stands, walkers assisting a few, Clive
Marshall moves his wheel chair over to Captain
Thomas.

                    CLIVE MARSHALL
        I had no idea I was so behind in my
        bills, I was going to be next in
        line after Lila. I'd probably be
        sleeping in the streets, this came
                    just in time.

                    CAPTAIN THOMAS
        I think in the long run, this will
            solve a lot of our problems.

Clive salutes the Captains and follows the others
out of the lounge area.

Captain Thomas and Captain Brooks turn to look at
the TV.

CLOSE UP OF TV SCREEN - KAMILLA HARRISON (50's)
the newly elected Governor of California steps up
to a podium with a microphone.

                    KAMILLA HARRISON
        I've been informed of this robbery
        this afternoon and it leaves me no
        doubt in my mind (a beat) the age
        of these two suspects clearly
        resonates with my campaign that got
        me elected as your Governor of
        California. I want to reiterate
        again, I will continue to do
        everything I can to make sure our
        retired community is safe and it is
        the responsibility of the state of
        California to provide and take
        better care of our senior citizens.

Captain Thomas and Captain Brooks look at each other, impressed with the media.

> CAPTAIN THOMAS
> Lila really did it. She started something.

A MOMENT.

> CAPTAIN BROOKS
> Did she ever sing that song to you?
> (singing to the tune
> "Anything you can do, I
> can do better")
> "Anything boys can do, girls can do better."

> CAPTAIN THOMAS
> (singing)
> "Girls can do anything better than boys."

> CAPTAIN BROOKS
> No, they can't!

> CAPTAIN THOMAS
> Yes, they can.

> CAPTAIN BROOKS
> No, they can't!

> CAPTAIN THOMAS
> Yes, they can!

> CAPTAIN BROOKS
> No, they can't!

> CAPTAIN BROOKS AND CAPTAIN THOMAS
> (still singing)
> Yes they can! Yes they can! Yes they can!

They both CHUCKLE a little. A MOMENT, thinking of their Lila.

> CAPTAIN BROOKS
> I'm sure going to miss her.

> CAPTAIN THOMAS
> Affirmative. (a beat) Me too.

Captain Thomas and Captain Brooks walk towards their rooms.

EXT. BEACH - SUNRISE - NEXT DAY

Michelle finishes putting back on her running clothes, she has just finished her daily run and emerged from her morning dip.

A BEACH PATROL SUV has driven down the beach and interrupts Michelle's morning ritual. MR. BEACH CONTROL gets out of his SUV with his ticket book.

> MR. BEACH PATROL
> Nudity is not allowed on public beaches.

Michelle looks around at the empty beach.

> MICHELLE
> There's no one around. And I'm not naked.

> MR. BEACH PATROL
> Your drivers license.

> MICHELLE
> I'm out running. I don't have my license on me.

> MR. BEACH PATROL
> (lifting his ticket book and pen)
> Name?

                    MICHELLE
        You're giving me a ticket? I have
                my clothes on!

                MR. BEACH PATROL
        Mam, in the state of California you
        need to have identification with
            you at all times. Name?

                    MICHELLE
            Lila. Lila Simmons.
                MR. BEACH PATROL
                Address?

                    MICHELLE
        100 Green Street. Venice.

Mr. Beach Patrol hands Michelle the ticket and he
goes back to his SUV.

                MICHELLE (CONT'D)
            Officer... One question?

Mr. Beach Patrol stops before getting in and
looks at Michelle.

                MICHELLE (CONT'D)
        Is it against the law to call you
                pathetic?

                MR. BEACH PATROL
                ...No it's not.

                    MICHELLE
            Thank you. Have a nice day.

The Beach Patrol leaves. Michelle runs past a
beach garbage can, crumples the ticket and throws
it away.

INT. RETIREMENT BUS - MORNING

The field trip bus is packed with the same group of Elders we have seen in 100 Green Street and also around the table in he Activity Lounge. The Captains get on the bus and take their seats at the front.

JANE BROWN, the Plaza's activity organizer gets on the bus. Rick, the bus driver looks up from the driver's seat. Jane Brown takes the bus microphone.

                    JANE BROWN
          Good morning everyone! Is everyone
          happy today? It was a scary day for
          all of us yesterday. You all left
               before I got on the bus.

Jane gives the bus driver Rick a friendly punch in the arm.

                JANE BROWN (CONT'D)
          No more long trips to wrong
                    destinations.
               (lifting a diabetic
                  emergency kit)
          And no more sugar lows for our
                  sweet bus driver.
             (she's clapping and getting
                everyone to join in)
          Let's hear it for Rick everyone,
             our wonderful bus driver!

Everyone on the bus CLAPS for the overly enthusiastic activities supervisor.

Captain Brooks speaks quietly to Captain Thomas.

                  CAPTAIN BROOKS
          She's cast overboard at the first
                      stop

                  CAPTAIN THOMAS
             Over and out Captain.

                    JANE BROWN
                   (to everyone)
          Now fasten those seat belts and get
               ready for a flowers day!

Sara Stanley sits next to Clive Marshall.

                   SARA STANLEY
                 What did she say?

                  CLIVE MARSHALL
           She said go change the world and
               make it a better place.

Sara smiles and puts her head back for a little
nap. Clive takes a pill and sits back to prepare
for the time of his life.

Rick closes the door; as happy Jane finds her
seat.

TAP TAP TAP! Mr. Mizrahi stands on the outside of
the bus wanting to come in.

Rick opens the door again. Mr. Mizrahi steps onto
the bus, kippah atop his head and walking cane in
his hand.

                    MR. MIZRAHI
                   (to everyone)
           Nothings here for me now. Is there
                   a seat for me?

Captain Thomas jumps up and helps him sit in the
last empty seat. Off they go. First stop...
Botanical gardens.

EXT. MICHELLE'S NEIGHBORHOOD - LATER

Michelle walks along the street. Her Angry
Neighbor is in his front yard. He motions
Michelle to come over.

                    ANGRY NEIGHBOR
            I need a moment with you!

Michelle isn't in the mood to speak with him but
she goes anyway. The Angry Neighbor is staring
and pointing at all his empty outdoor potted
plants.

                ANGRY NEIGHBOR (CONT'D)
                She took them all!

Michelle doesn't understand what the neighbor is
taking about.

                    MICHELLE
        I'm not following. What are you
                talking about.

                    ANGRY NEIGHBOR
        Sorry... I'm She's dug up all my
                God damn flowers!

Michelle's expression changes, she realizes that
her freshly planted pots are her neighbors stolen
flowers.

                    MICHELLE
        Ah... I'm... sorry. I don't know.

                    ANGRY NEIGHBOR
        She's sleeping on your doorstep.
            Did you not know that too?

Michelle begins to walk back to her apartment.

                ANGRY NEIGHBOR (CONT'D)
                I'm on to you two!

EXT. MICHELLE'S APARTMENT

Michelle stops on her doorstep, looking down at
her colorful freshly potted plants. Martha, the
homeless woman has not only been sleeping on her

doorstep but has been doing some night gardening at Michelle's house.

> MICHELLE
> (to herself)
> I thought something looked better
> around here.
> Michelle fluffs the pillow on the chair next to
> the door and
> goes inside.

EXT. BOTANICAL GARDENS - LATER

The PLAZA BUS pulls up in front of the entrance.

INT. RETIREMENT BUS - CONTINUOUS

Jane Brown stands.

> JANE BROWN
> Easy does it everyone. Use the
> handrail as we get off the bus
> single file.

Jane Brown gets off the bus. VIVIANE WILSON (80's) stands quickly and faces everyone.

> VIVIANE WILSON
> I... can't. I'm...sorry...I still
> have my kids, grandkids...they'd
> have a fit if I went through with
> it. Good luck everyone.

The Residents on the bus understand. A few wave good-bye to her as she gets off the bus.

Captain Brooks and Captain Thomas stand quickly and face everyone.

> CAPTAIN BROOKS
> Last Chance?

> CAPTAIN THOMAS
> We're already behind schedule.

Everyone is in for the ride.

> SARA STANLEY
> What did he say?

> CLIVE MARSHALL
> Last stop before Disneyland.

Sara smiles in awe of the Captains.

> SARA STANLEY
> Those Captains have such a sense of
> humor.

Rick closes the door and off they go once again.

EXT. BOTANICAL GARDENS - CONTINUOUS

Jane Brown is speechless as she watches the bus
drive away.

> JANE BROWN
> Again! Where the hell do they think
> they're going this time.

> VIVIANE WILSON
> They're going to the toy store.

Jane rolls her eyes at this.

> JANE BROWN
> They are my responsibility!
> (taking out her cellphone)
> I'm calling the plaza.

> VIVIANE WILSON
> Nonsense honey!
> (tempting her)
> I know this place. They make a
> great martini in the garden
> restaurant.

Jane Brown is distracted now; she loves her martinis. Jane puts her phone away. Vivianne and Jane walk towards the garden gates.

EXT. STREETS OF WEST LOS ANGELES - MORNING - LATER

The Plaza bus pulls over on the same street corner that Michelle met Harold a few days before.

INT. RETIREMENT PLAZA - CONTINUOUS

Captain Thomas and Captain Brooks greet Harold as he steps up on the bus.

> CAPTAIN THOMAS
> Sorry we're late.

> CAPTAIN BROOKS
> We had to get rid of the one too many deckhands.

> HAROLD
> You're only one minute late. (a beat) If you take the freeway East, take Robertson exit, it opens at ten.

Harold and the Captains take their seat. The bus door closes.

> RICK KENT
> (into bus microphone)
> Next stop! Toys'r Us everyone!

Everyone on the bus CLAPS enthusiastically, a few CHEERS.

INT. MICHELLE'S APARTMENT

Michelle checks her home answering machine.

> ANSWERING MACHINE
> (computerized voice)
> You have no messages.

Michelle checks her cell phone, she has one message.

> MEL (O.S.)
> Hi it's Mel. Just wanted to wish you a good morning. No message from my dad. He usually calls me every morning. Not sure if that's the case with your dad. Can't say that I'm relaxed about all of this. But...well...just wanted to thank you for yesterday and... well... maybe we could grab...lunch sometime? A proper introduction. Well... you have my number. I'll probably see you around the plaza.

Michelle smiles.

> MICHELLE
> (to herself)
> Just ask me for lunch scaredy cat.

She heads towards the shower.

EXT. TOYS R US - LATER

> The Plaza bus has pulled up at the front entrance. Everyone for the bus is in a group meeting, some with walkers, Clive is in his wheelchair.

The two Captains, Harold and Rick the bus driver stand at the front of the group.

             CAPTAIN THOMAS
        We have ten minutes everyone.

             CAPTAIN BROOKS
       Buy your weapon and return to the
              bus immediately.

Everyone nods "yes" and begins to file inside.

             SARA STANLEY
           What's he saying?

            CLIVE MARSHALL
        They have a great Ninja sword.

             SARA STANLEY
       Would wonder woman use a ninja
                 sword?

            CLIVE MARSHALL
          That would be so hot!

Following the group, Sara is excitedly pushes
Clive into the store in his wheelchair.

          INT. PARTY CITY - LATER

The group from the bus enter a warehouse style
costume store led by the two Captains, Harold and
Rick. A quick meeting once again.

             CAPTAIN THOMAS
         You have ten minutes. Find your
              disguise everyone.

             CAPTAIN BROOKS
       A wide variety here. Get creative.

          Every nods "yes."

             CLIVE OWENS
       I've always wanted to be Robin
                 hood.

>   (to Sara Stanley)
>   Let's go Wonder woman.

Sara is like a schoolgirl, looking up at all the colorful costumes. She pushes Clive in his wheelchair down an aisle. Everyone else excitedly disperse to what seems to be an endless number of costume aisles.

INT. BANK OF AMERICA - LATER

Michelle enters as Chuck Harris is placing an empty box on her desk. She approaches her desk and looks inside the box.

>   MICHELLE
>   What's this for?

>   CHUCK HARRIS
>   You are going on a leave of absence
>   until the investigation of the
>   robbery is concluded.

>   MICHELLE
>   Why don't you just fire me.

>   CHUCK HARRIS
>   Michelle you have to look where the
>   cards lie. All the facts are
>   pointing at you and your new
>   boyfriend.

>   MICHELLE
>   Is this about me not wanting to
>   sleep with you anymore?

Michelle stares at him in disbelief. Michelle steps in closer, lowering her voice.

>   MICHELLE (CONT'D)
>   Stop fucking with me, Chuck.

Chuck looks around and up to the surveillance camera. He angles his back towards the surveillance camera, reaches down and unzips his fly.

> CHUCK HARRIS
> You know you want this and you were
> so good at it.

Michelle smiles, stepping in closer.

> MICHELLE
> Yes...I was.

Chuck looks around making sure everyone is busy.

> CHUCK HARRIS
> (tempting her)
> Touch it.

Michelle reaches inside his unzipped fly and grabs his manly part. Chuck closes his eyes. Chucks eyes open wide when she gives him a hard yank. Chuck falls to the ground in pain.

Now everyone's looking at Chuck on the ground.

> CHUCK HARRIS (CONT'D)
> AHHHHHHHHHH!

> MICHELLE
> Just in case a bank robbery isn't
> enough to get me fired.

Michelle grabs her bag and laptop and leaves.

EXT. WESTWOOD BLVD/FIRST GRUNION BANK - LATER

The Plaza bus pulls up along the curb in front of First Grunion Bank.

INT. RETIREMENT BUS - CONTINUOUS
The two Captains stand at the front of the bus.

> CAPTAIN THOMAS
> This is it everyone.

> CAPTAIN BROOKS
> Are we all clear with the plan of
> action?

Everyone nods "yes" as we reveal the bus occupants, instead of the group of Retired Passengers, we see what looks to be a masquerade party of cartoon characters. Harold stands putting on a, "Kermit the Frog" mask. He even found a green T-shirt to go with the look. A masked "Miss Piggy" blonde wig, long black gloves and pearls stands follows. The masked Muppet critics, "Statler and Waldorf" follow behind.

The Muppets shake the two Captains hands and leave the bus.

Captain Thomas stops Waldorf before he exits, takes Waldorf's gun out of his hand and removes the "Toys r Us" tag off.

> CAPTAIN THOMAS
> What was the last thing Lila said
> to us?

> EVERYONE
> Check your weapons.

> CAPTAIN BROOKS
> Team! This is important. We must
> look professional.

Waldorf gets his gun back and exits the bus.

EXT. WESTWOOD BLVD - CONTINUOUS

FIRST GRUNION BANK

The Plaza Bus doors close and moves towards the
next stop, leaving Kermit, Miss Piggy, Statler
and Waldorf standing in a group on the sidewalk.

                    HAROLD/KERMIT
                (to his fellow Muppets)
            Hold tight everyone. Act normal.
            Just another day on the boulevard.

A few PEDESTRIANS walk by staring at the MUPPETS
hanging out
on the sidewalk. The Pedestrians wave and the
Muppets wave
back. Everyone loves the Muppets.

BANK OF LOS ANGELES - MOMENTS LATER

The Plaza bus pulls up in front of the next bank.
The "Three
Little Pigs" get off the bus and move around
quickly to the
back of the bus.

The Three Pigs open the back doors of the bus,
Clive, "The
Big Bad Wolf" wheel chair bound is lowered to the
sidewalk.
Doors are closed the Plaza bus leaves the Three
Pigs and a
Wolf on the sidewalk.

FIRST TRUST OF SANTA MONICA

The Plaza bus pulls up in front of the third
bank.

INT. PLAZA BUS - CONTINUOUS

Captain Brooks stands at the front of the bus,
it's his stop.
Captain Thomas is driving. Rick, the bus driver
is already
gone, he was one of the Three Pigs.

CAPTAIN BROOKS
(to Captain Thomas)
Damn it! I'm beginning to have
doubts myself. I don't think I've
been this crazy nervous since I hit
the reef back in the 1970's.

CAPTAIN THOMAS
We all make mistakes. You are a
fine Captain.

The two Captains smile at each other. Captain
Brooks straps a
long beard around his face, a patch over his eye
and places
his white Captains hat back on his head.

CAPTAIN BROOKS
Always wanted to Pirate a ship.

Captain Brooks lifts his hand which is now a
hook. Captain
Thomas shakes the hook. They step back and salute
each other.

CAPTAIN THOMAS
Go get'em Hook!

Captain Hook leaves the bus, followed by Peter
Pan, Tinker
Bell and the Alligator. (Party City has
everything)

Captain Thomas closes the doors of the bus and
drives ahead.

CAPTAIN THOMAS (CONT'D)
Be ready team. Last stop.

EXT. WESTWOOD BLVD/WELLS FORGET BANK

The Plaza bus pulls up in front of the fourth bank. Doors
open, Sara steps off the bus, eyeing her surroundings. Wonder
Woman is checking to see if the coast is clear. Iron Man
steps off the bus but misses the last step, masks don't
always let you see perfectly. Robin gets off the bus and
helps Wonder Woman get Iron Man back on his feet.

INT. PLAZA BUS - SAME TIME

Captain Thomas is dressed in a Batman suit. He stands over
Mr. Mizrahi who is sound asleep in his seat. Captain Thomas
removes his Captain's hat and places it on Mr. Mizrahi's lap.

CAPTAIN THOMAS
Take care of this for me my friend.
It's been a tough couple of days
for you.

EXT. WESTWOOD BLVD/WELLS FORGET BANK

BATMAN, cape, mask and all jumps off the bus and looks
around. Captain Thomas makes a fine super hero. The others
move in next to him.

SARA STANLEY/WONDER WOMAN
(to Batman)
You look fantastic!

CAPTAIN THOMAS/BATMAN
Thanks Wonder woman. It was a toss
up between Superman and --

ROBIN
I couldn't have done it without you
Batman.

They all agree. A MOMENT before...

CAPTAIN THOMAS/BATMAN
Tell me where the trigger is?

Batman, Robin, Wonder woman and Ironman calk
their plastic guns and walk towards the doors of
the bank.

FIRST TRUST OF SANTA MONICA

Captain Hook, Peter Pan, Tinker Bell and the
Alligator calk their plastic guns.

CAPTAIN BROOKS/CAPTAIN HOOK
There's no stopping. Our fingers are on the
trigger.

They walk towards the bank doors.

BANK OF LOS ANGELES

The Big Bad Wolf and the Three Pigs calk their
plastic guns.

CLIVE MARSHALL/BIG BAD WOLF
We'll huff and we'll puff and we'll blow them all
down.
The wheel-chaired Wolf and Three Pigs head into
the bank.

FIRST GRUNION BANK

Kermit, Miss Piggy, Statler and Waldorf have been
waiting the longest for everyone else from the
bus to be dropped off at their banks. TOURISTS
have been keeping them busy with photos
on the sidewalk. Miss Piggy is in character as
she poses seductively.

Trying to get everyone to get their plan of action together,

Harold/Kermit lifts his gun in the air. Tourists SCREAM and run away from the scene.

Miss Piggy, Statler and Waldorf aim their plastic guns. More SCREAMS from PEDESTRIANS.

> HAROLD/KERMIT
> Life's like a movie, write your own ending.

The Muppets move towards the bank and enter.

INT. GROCERY STORE - SAME TIME

Mel stands in a long line of IMPATIENT SHOPPERS at the Cashier counter once again. He notices Virginia Jones is back at the grocery store and is at the front of the line with a few items on the conveyer belt.
(Michelle and Mel gave her money to buy the Pez candy for her grandson a few days before.) Virginia is looking through her purse for more money.

> CASHIER
> Mam, I'll need your savings card.

Mel moves up to the front of the line and gives the Cashier his savings card.

> MEL
> Swipe mine. She said last time she doesn't have one.

> The Cashier swipes the card.

> CASHIER
> Mam, we are short on cashiers today, is there any way you can--

Virginia looks up with a handgun pointed at the
Cashier. She waves it at Mel and everyone else to
step back. Virginia moves her purse towards the
Cashier.

                    VIRGINIA
                    (to Mel)
         Sorry sonny. Today I need a little
              more than a savings card.
                 (to the Cashier)
                  Fill it up.

The Cashier starts to fill Virginia's purse and
then stops.

                    CASHIER
          Wait a minute. You've been watching
           the news about the two old ladies
                  robbing the bank.

                    VIRGINIA
            That's right... Smart girls if you
                     ask me.

                    CASHIER
             That's a plastic gun. You can't
           fool me, I know a plastic gun when
                     I see--

Virginia aims her gun at a Balloon advertisement
above the Cashiers head and CLICK! Pulls the
trigger. BANG!

Mel and everyone else in the line-up hits the
floor. Virginia points the gun back at the
Cashier.

                    VIRGINIA
            I'm sorry sweetheart. I didn't hear
           everything you just said. Could you
                   repeat that?

Needless to say, the Cashier continues to fill
Virginia's purse.

INT. WESTWOOD BLVD BANKS - AT THE SAME TIME

A SERIES OF CAMERA SHOTS OF THE REACTIONS OF BANK
EMPLOYEES AS THE FOUR BANKS ARE HELD AT GUNPOINT.
HANDS HELD HIGH IN THE AIR IN ALL FOR BANKS, OUR
TEAM OF MUPPETS, THE THREE LITTLE PIGS AND THE
WOLF, CAPTAIN HOOK'S TEAM AND SUPER HEROES AIM
THEIR GUNS.

A SERIES OF CLOSE UP SHOTS OF TELLERS FEET
STEPPING ON EMERGENCY BUTTONS TO NOTIFY POLICE.

WELLS FORGET BANK

Robin, Wonder woman, and Ironman stand by with
guns pointed at CUSTOMERS and other EMPLOYEES.
Ironman turns and bumps into a deposit desk, he
can't see a damn thing with that mask. Captain
Thomas/Batman, with gun pointed approaches a
YOUNG WOMAN TELLER. He passes her a Batman Party
bag.

                    CAPTAIN THOMAS/BATMAN
              Hello darling. Have you called for
                        the police yet?

The YOUNG TELLER is petrified. She can barely
shake her head "No."

                    CAPTAIN THOMAS/BATMAN (CONT'D)
                    (calmly, putting her at
                        ease)
              The emergency peddle should be just
                  under your foot. Go ahead. And
              while you're doing that, just put a
                  little cash in the bag. (a beat)
                    What a lovely dress.
                    BANK OF LOS ANGELES

Clive/Bad Wolf is in his wheelchair with his gun
raised at a a MALE TELLER. The Teller is having a
hard time seeing the robber because he's sitting
low his wheelchair.

112

                    MALE TELLER
    Are you sure that's a real gun you
                    got there?
    It was the First Lady and Hilary
    bank robbery yesterday and today's
        the big bad wolf and little red
                    riding hood.

                 CLIVE/BAD WOLF
    Wrong story. Didn't your parents
            ever read to you?

Pig/Mr. Mizrahi points his cane with the other
two Pigs and their guns, he makes his way up to
Clive/Bad Wolf.

                 MR.MIZRAHI/PIG
    I'm going to have to make a quick
            trip to the bathroom.

EXT. WESTWOOD BLVD - CONTINUOUS

Four bank robberies on the same street have
successfully notified 911. The mayhem of Police
cars, squat teams, News Teams and helicopters
fighting for their territory in the sky create
the scene of what you think could only be
imagined. All four banks are in the process of
being surrounded.

Sgt. John Doe shows up in his car and jumps out.

                  SGT. JOHN DOE
    Get everything closed off! I don't
    want to see anyone on this street.
        More back up is on it's way.

Sgt. John Doe is joined by the LAPD CAPTAIN.

                  LAPD CAPTAIN
    I thought I'd seen everything.

                    SGT. JOHN DOE
        I said that yesterday. What do we
                        got?

                    CAPTAIN LAPD
        All suspects are still in the
        building. Four banks are covered.
        One phone call from the manager at
        First Grunion bank said something
            about Kermit the frog.

SGT. John Doe takes a MOMENT.

                    SGT.JOHN DOE
        I've got a hunch, that these guys
            are asking to get caught.

EXT. MICHELLE'S APARTMENT - SAME TIME

Michelle walks up the stairs. On her front
doorstep, Touli and Georgie, the homeless cat and
three legged dog sleeping in a box. Michelle
looks around. Martha is nowhere in sight.

                    MICHELLE
        Please don't tell me my life has
        just become further complicated.

Michelle picks up a note left next to the animals
and reads it.

                MICHELLE (CONT'D)
                (reading note)
            Just what I thought.

The animals look up at her in a half slumber.

                MICHELLE (CONT'D)
        Touli and Georgie. Come on in you
                        two.

Michelle opens her door. Touli and Georgie follow
her inside.

INT. MICHELLE'S APARTMENT - CONTINUOUS

Michelle turns the TV onto the News and heads
into the kitchen to put down a bowl of water for
the animals.

                    TV NEWS BROADCAST (O.S.)
             There has been an unusual number of
             robberies reported since yesterdays
               bank robbery which is now being
             referred to as "First Ladies Bank
                 Heist." It seems the robbery
                performed by two women, know as
             Lila Simmons and Delia Zamora, both
              senior citizens might have sparked
              what LAPD officials are calling a
                retirement renegade (a beat) one
              moment everyone...we have a just
                had news reported by our live
                 coverage team... three banks
                 are...I'm sorry, four banks on
              Westwood Boulevard are currently
                   being held up, as we
             speak...suspects are still in the
              banks and it is unknown how many
                    people are involved...

Michelle is moving quickly towards the TV,
followed by her new pets.

EXT. WESTWOOD BLVD - SAME TIME

LAPD have their weapons aimed. Helicopters hover
overhead. Squat teams take their mark, ready for
the suspects to appear out of the banks. The LAPD
seems to have deployed their entire Police Force
to this location. The city is on lock down and
now it waits. News Teams are ready...

Sgt. John Doe stands with the LAPD Captain.

SGT. JOHN DOE
(over loud speaker)
Come out with your hands up! You
are surrounded. No one gets hurt
if you drop your weapons and come
out with your hands up!

SILENCE

SGT. JOHN DOE (CONT'D)
I repeat! Come out with--

The doors of the Banks slowly open
simultaneously. CLICK! CLICK! CLICK! LAPD and
SQUAT TEAM calk their weapons.

Our group of cartoon characters emerge from each
bank with their hands held high in the air.

LAW ENFORCEMENT moves in.

SGT. JOHN DOE (CONT'D)
Get down on the ground. Keep your
hands in the air, get down on your
knees and lie on the ground.

Our cartoon convicts have a small problem. They
are all in an age range from 80-90, they need
their hands to get down to the ground. They try
but don't get very far.

WELLS FORGET BANK

LAPD moves in towards Batman.

LAPD OFFICER 2
Get down on the ground! Now!

CAPTAIN THOMAS/BATMAN
Son... we need are hands for that
maneuver. Joints don't move like
they use to.

LAPD OFFICER 2 takes a MOMENT before really understanding the situation. He looks to his partner, LAPD OFFICER 1.

> LAPD OFFICER 2
> Cover me.

LAPD OFFICER 2 runs over to Sgt. John Doe and LAPD Captain.

> LAPD OFFICER 2 (CONT'D)
> Sarge. I think it's the Retirement Renegade part two. They're gonna need their hands to get to the ground.

Sgt. John Doe looks at LAPD Captain.

> SGT. JOHN DOE
> Just when I thought I'd seen it all.

> LAPD CAPTAIN
> You said that yesterday.

> SGT. JOHN DOE
> (into loud speaker)
> You all may use your hands. Move slowly. I repeat, move slowly to the ground.

> LAPD CAPTAIN
> I don't think the word slowly is necessary on this one.

Our group of Cartoon characters move as slowly as you would expect someone in their age range to move to the ground.

INT. MICHELLE'S APARTMENT - SAME TIME

Michelle is watching the LIVE COVERAGE OF THE BANK HEIST ON TV. Her cellphone rings.

> MICHELLE
> (into phone)
> Have you seen what's going on in
> Westwood?

> MEL (O.S.)
> No... but you're never gonna guess
> who just robbed the grocery store.
> Do you remember when--

Michelle's eyes widen a little more, her eyes
have been on the TV SCREEN the entire time.

> MICHELLE
> (into phone)
> Holy Fuck!

EXT. WESTWOOD BLVD/WELLS FORGET BANK - SAME TIME

LAPD OFFICER 2 has Batman and his superhero
friends in handcuffs.

> CAPTAIN THOMAS/BATMAN
> Son...I'm getting a little
> claustrophobic, would you be so
> kind as to take my mask off for me.

The News Team moves in closer catching the live
coverage.

The LAPD Officer obliges.

INT. MICHELLE'S APARTMENT - SAME TIME

Michelle is speechless.

> MEL (O.S.)
> What's going on Michelle?

EXT. WESTWOOD BLVD - SAME TIME

The LAPD OFFICERS now have our Cartoon Criminals in handcuffs. They are all in a group, handcuffed and disguises have been removed.

The News Team is right up front, cameras taking in every moment.

INT. MICHELLE'S APARTMENT - SAME TIME

Michelle is now sitting on the floor, phone at her ear, staring, almost crying in disbelief at the TV SCREEN. Touli and Georgie have made themselves a comfortable spot on her lap.

                    MEL (O.S.)
          Michelle! What's is it? What's
              going on? Are you okay?

                    MICHELLE
          Ah...it's been a hard fucking day.
          You need to come over? I need to
                  tell you something.

Michelle continues to stare at the Live News Coverage, as she pets Touli and Georgie in her lap.

INT. COURTHOUSE/SENTENCING HEARING 1 - THREE WEEKS LATER

JUDGE FRED GREEN (80's) sits at the front of the room.

                    JUDGE GREEN
          You do realize, by the law of State
                of California, I have no
            alternative but to give you both
            minimal punishment of seven years?

Lila Simmons and Delia Zamora stand, handcuffed, dressed in inmate overalls at the front of the court room.

                    LILA
          Yes, your honor.

                    DELIA
          Yes, your honor.

We see News Media capturing their trial, Michelle and Mel sit together amongst the full courthouse.

                 JUDGE GREEN
          Do you have anything you want to
            say to the court before your
                 imposing sentence?

Lila steps forward.

                    LILA
          I have lived in America all my
          life. I have lived in a country
             that has made me proud.

                    DELIA
          But why is it that a citizen, at
          our age has to commit a crime to
          raise attention... The system is
          failing us. As we grow older we
          become what happens to us. The
          narrative of what the American
             dream stands for has been
          forgotten. There are third world
          countries that take better care of
          our citizens. I was ready to die
          for this country. At my age, we are
          looked upon as a burden if we don't
          have money. Respect for the elderly
             has fallen to the waste side.
          Why get excited about a senior
          citizen discount when on the inside
          it's for free. I have celebrated
          Independence day for the last 85

years of my life, today I celebrate
the day I will feel the worry of
survival gone. You have left us no
choice. We are all one pay-cheque
away from being homeless.

COURTHOUSE/SENTENCING HEARING 2

Harold and the Three other Retired Citizens from
the Westwood Blvd bus (The Muppets) stand in
handcuffs and inmate clothing. Harold has stepped
forward; he has something to say before his
sentencing.

                    HAROLD
        I served in World War 2, I was
        ready to die for this country. My
        days of running when I was a young
        boy took me to the Olympics. I was
        proud to say I represented United
        States of America. (a beat) My legs
          have tired your honor, with no
        money I am a burden to society. My
        circumstances left me no choice...

COURTHOUSE/SENTENCING HEARING 3

Judge Green sits at his bench. The courtroom
seems even more crowded. News Teams getting every
MOMENT on live coverage.
Clive Marshall sits in his wheelchair, the three
other Retired Citizens stand next to him in
handcuffs and jumpsuits.

                  CLIVE MARSHALL
        I have celebrated Independence Day
        for as long as I can remember. It
        meant Freedom. When you're young
           Independent has a different
        meaning. It's easier to take care
        of yourself. I'm dependent on my
        country to take care of me now...

COURTHOUSE/SENTENCING HEARING 4
Virginia from the grocery story stands in
handcuffs and a inmate jumpsuit.

                    VIRGINIA
          Who in their right mind wouldn't
          commit a crime and know they can
            get three meals a day on the
            inside...you think I want to be
          cutting god damned coupons for the
            rest of my god damned life!?

(O.S.) We hear LAUGHTER in the courthouse.

Judge Green BANGS his gavel down on his desk.

                   JUDGE GREEN
            (he's somewhat amused too)
          Order in the court. You may
                   continue.

                    VIRGINIA
          I'm suppose to get excited for a
          senior discount, when I know for a
            fact, because I've done my
            research...on the inside
            everything's for free.

COURTHOUSE/SENTENCING HEARING 5

Martha, the homeless woman that left her pets on
Michelle's doorstep stands in handcuffs and an
inmate jumpsuit.

                    MARTHA
            Losing my garden killed me more
            than losing my house. If you're a
          gardener, you'd understand that. I
            just need dirt, seeds, sun, water
          and time. Where you're sending me,
                  can I have that?

122

COURTHOUSE/SENTENCING HEARING 6

Captain Brooks stands with the three other Retired Citizens from his Captain Hook bank robbery. They are handcuffed and in jumpsuits.

Captain Brooks has stepped forward.

> CAPTAIN BROOKS
> The narrative of what the American
> dream stands for has been
> forgotten. Where's the American
> pie?
> (starts off talking but
> can't resist to evolve
> into singing it)
> When the jester sang for the king
> and queen, in a coat he borrowed
> from James Dean. And a voice that
> came from you and me, Oh and while
> the King was looking down, The
> jester stole his thorny crown. The
> courtroom was adjourned: No verdict
> was returned. And while Lenin read
> a book of Marx, the quartet
> practiced in the park. And we sang
> dirges in the dark the day the
> music died. We were singing... "Bye
> bye Miss American pie."

The courthouse can't resist but to join in for one more time.
Michelle and Mel look around at what looks like courthouse karaoke. They've been at every trial and hearing, exhaustion lowers their resistance and they join in.

> EVERYONE IN THE COURTHOUSE
> Drove my chevy to the levee but the
> levee was dry. Them good ole boys
> were drinkin' whisky and rye and
> singin', "this'll be the day that I
> die. This'll be the day that I
> die." We were singing..."Bye-bye--

Judge Green was getting into it too but authority calls. He
BANGS his gavel.

COURTHOUSE/SENTENCING HEARING 7

Captain Thomas stands with Sara, (hearing problem), Rick, (the bus driver) and the other Retired Citizen who was Iron Man in the robbery.

> CAPTAIN THOMAS
> I speak for myself and also for the retired population of the United States. (a beat) We live in a country that prides itself on respect and honor. So why is it that our country can't guarantee a simple pillow under our heads when we take our last breath as an American citizen? (a beat) That's all, your honor.

The courtroom stirs uncomfortably.

Judge Green stares at the courtroom. Affected by his weeks of trials and sentencing.

> JUDGE GREEN
> This is the last day that I will sit as a Judge of this court. I had thought that this would be a day of reflection on the conclusion of a Judicial Career that had brought me a sense of satisfaction and sense of completion of service to the law and society. Instead I will remember this day as a day of infamy. I have been required by the Criminal law of this State to sentence 24 elderly men and women otherwise law abiding American citizens, who have spent their productive lives contributing to

the welfare of this country to
imprisonment for robbery. They have
raised families, paid taxes and
contributed to their communities.
Now in the twilight of their lives
they, as a result of the social
policies of the wealthiest country
in the world, find themselves with
no ability to house, feed or obtain
necessary medical services. Robbery
with or without a weapon (in these
cases an imitation pistol) is a
serious offense and should not be
tolerated by any society. Our state
has decreed that on conviction for
such an offense the minimum
sentence is to be seven years-no
exceptions. This in my view
constitutes cruel and unusual
punishment and is the idiocy on
full display, of mandated minimum
sentences, that take away the
sentencing discretion of learned
and experienced Judges. Shame on
the legislators of this country and
state for their social and legal
irresponsibility. I can only hope
these cases will force a rethink of
this ill advised draconian
legislation.
(banging gavel on desk)
Court dismissed.

Judge Green stands and leaves.

The Courtroom ERUPTS INTO CHAOS. Captain Thomas,
Rick, Sara and the Two Retired Citizens from the
fourth bank robbery are led out by the Deputy
Sheriff.

SARA STANLEY
(to Captain Thomas)
What's he say?

                    CAPTAIN THOMAS
          We got seven years to get you and
           United States of America a better
                    hearing aid.

TWO MONTHS LATER

INT. WOMEN'S CALIFORNIA STATE PRISON/CAFETERIA -
MORNING

Lila, Delia, Martha, Vivianne, Sara and a few
other Retired Women that committed the bank
robberies, stand in long line of INMATES to
collect their breakfast. CRYSTAL DRAKE (50's)
stands in the front of the line and nods a
"morning" to LYNDA AXELL (50's), and BEATRICE
OWENS (40's) as they join the line.

                    VIVIANE WILSON
          The one thing that doesn't change
           in this country is the God Damn
           lines. (a beat) At least they ain't
            going to ask me for that savings
          card. Scrummaging through my purse,
                    dig, dig, dig...

                       CRYSTAL
           Can we keep it quiet? No one cares
               about the outside in here.

Viviane makes a little face towards Crystal's
back.

                    VIVIANE WILSON
                     (impressed)
            How can someone younger be more
                   grouchy than me.

Lila shifts in her step; her hip is bugging her.

                        DELIA
            Sit down. I'll bring you your food.

                    MARTHA
        The food could probably walk there
                    itself.

The Retired Ladies LAUGH a little. Crystal turns
around and gives them all a look.

                MARTHA (CONT'D)
        That's gonna change here very soon.

                    CRYSTAL
        Just wait, this place will give you
        nothing to laugh about before long.

                    LILA
        After next week's surgery, I'll be
                    partying.

Chrystal steps back, knocking Sara with her tray.
Chrystal's tray falls to the floor.

                    CRYSTAL
        Hey! Watch it! It's called space
                    old woman!

It was Chrystal mishap, but everyone else moves
in to clean up the mess.

                    SARA
        Of course there's space at our
        table. Come join us. What's your
                    name dearie?

            Crystal ignores Sara.

                    LILA
        Her name is Crystal. What happened
            to catching butterflies?

Crystal looks at Lila with a look of familiarity.
Lila was a principle school teacher and she never
forgot a young student. Lila passes her tray to
Crystal.

> LILA (CONT'D)
> Take mine.

INT. MEN'S CA STATE PRISON/VISITING ROOM - SAME
TIME

CAUCASIAN, MEXICAN, AFRICAN AMERICAN, AMERICAN
INDIAN, the full range of INMATES wait in line to
be served their breakfast. CRAZY HORSE (30's)
AMERICAN INDIAN, long hair, his tattoos tell us
he's spent a good part of his life in gangs
or detention facilities stands behind Harold.
They arrive in the line in front of the Two
Captains and breakfast is put on their trays.

> HAROLD
> (Harold smiles, he no
> longer has a front tooth
> missing)
> Captains! Top of the morning to you
> both.

> CAPTAIN BROOKS
> Wow! Look at that smile!

Harold is still smiling, he turns and taps his
right ear. He now has a hearing aid.

> HAROLD
> Man oh man! I can finally hear
> myself smile.

> CRAZY HORSE
> Hear this, Monkey Mouth! Move it
> along. I gotta shit before yard.

> HAROLD
> Go easy on that greasy thing over
> there.

> CRAZY HORSE
> Give me what he doesn't want.

CAPTAIN THOMAS
(holding a scoop of greasy
hash-browns)
That would be murder son. Too much
of this stuff will kill ya.

HAROLD
See you in the yard later.

An incredulous LAUGH from Crazy Horse, he walks
away with his tray. Harold follows.

HAROLD (CONT'D)
(to Crazy Horse)
What's your name son?

CRAZY HORSE
(bothered)
Crazy Horse.

HAROLD
Harold.

Crazy Horse can't be bothered to engage in
conversation, continuing to walk towards his
table with his food.

Back at the cafeteria line-up, Rick, the bus
driver and the other Retired Men from the
robberies make their way to collect their
breakfast. Clive in his wheelchair joins the
line.

CLIVE MARSHALL
(high-fives Rick and the
other retired guys)
Brothers! What's happening homey!

Clive is not only getting into the groove of
prison lingo but whips open his inmate jumpsuit
and flashes his new ink.

CLIVE MARSHALL (CONT'D)
Feast your eyes on this!

CLOSE-UP OF A TATOO ON HIS CHEST OF THE BIG BAD WOLF.

EXT. MEN'S CALIFORNIA STATE PRISON - LATER

Michelle and Mel stand in line with FAMILIES, FRIENDS and LEGAL COUNCIL outside the Guard gates leading into the prison. Handbags and personal belongings are placed on a conveyer belt. Michelle walks through the body scanner followed by Mel.

INT. MEN'S CA STATE PRISON/VISITING ROOM - MOMENTS LATER

It's a room where the inmates join with their families and friends on visiting hours. Picnic tables, vending machines line one wall. Michelle and Mel sit at a table with the Two Captains.

                    CAPTAIN THOMAS
          We've been watching the news in the
             evening. Looks like we really
                  started something.

                    CAPTAIN BROOKS
          They call us the "Retired Revolt"
                     in here.

                        MEL
          We've been watching too. Five more
            bank robberies in the last two
                      weeks.

                     MICHELLE
          We brought you guys something.

Mel presents Captain Brooks white hat. Captain Brooks holds his white hat as if it was a lover returned from the dead.

                        MEL
          The Jail Officer kept this for you,

wanted me to give it to you.

                    CAPTAIN BROOKS
              He was such a good chap. She's
                        back.

Captain Brooks places his life back on his head.
Michelle presents Captain Thomas's hat that he
left on the bus.

                      MICHELLE
              And Mr. Mizrahi wanted me to give
                     this to you.
                    (dumbfounded)
              Said he was sorry he fell asleep
              and disappointed he missed out on
              the opportunity. Anyway...he wants
              to come with us for a visit next
                        week.

Captain Thomas is almost in tears to have his hat
back. He places his life back on his head.

                    CAPTAIN THOMAS
                Now we have it all.

                    CAPTAIN BROOKS
                Couldn't ask for more.

                      MICHELLE
                    (in disbelief)
                    Have it all?

                        MEL
              Are we missing something here?

                      MICHELLE
              Wasn't it enough when mom spent
              time and we were back and forth
              every weekend to the woman's
              facility? I have to do this with my
                    father now?

131

Mel looks at Captain Brooks; they both are confused. Michelle and Captain Thomas realize they need to fill in the blanks on this one.

                    MICHELLE (CONT'D)
          When my mother had dementia, my
             father took her to Vegas...

                    CAPTAIN THOMAS
                Her one last WHOO-HAA...

                       MICHELLE
              She loved her gambling...

                    CAPTAIN THOMAS
               I left her alone for five
            minutes...came out...our life
             savings gone in one bet...

                       MICHELLE
          Turns out she wasn't happy about
                        that.

                    CAPTAIN THOMAS
           Neither was the casino when she
           held it up at gun point demanding
                  her money back.

                    A MOMENT.

                    CAPTAIN BROOKS
                All in five minutes?

                    CAPTAIN THOMAS
          Maybe seven, I got distracted by a
            pretty blonde at the Russian
                  roulette table.

                        MEL
            So all this is old hat for you
                        guys?

MICHELLE
(losing it, getting louder)
No! I mean seriously. I have no
job, I have a dad and all his
friends incarcerated for the next
seven years, already a good portion
of my 30's and now 40's are going
to be spent eating out of those
vending machines every weekend and
to top it all off... I just got a
sexual harassment case filed
against me!

They realize that got EVERYONE'S attention in the
room. SILENCE before all the INMATES start to
APPLAUD her. A WHISTLE is blown by a GUARD,
calming things down.

CAPTAIN BROOKS
They like a strong ambitious woman
in here.

CAPTAIN THOMAS
What in heavens name happened,
Michelle?

Michelle sits back, she can't believe her father
is actually in shock that she's faulted. The Two
Captains look at Mel.

MEL
What? It's not me. I'd welcome a
little sexual harassment.

CAPTAIN THOMAS
Chuck?

She nods "yes." They all look at her "asking what
she did."
Michelle takes a MOMENT before mimicking with her
hand "a reach, grab and pull." Needless to say
the two Captains and Mel's expression convey
compassion on Chuck's part.

133

                    CAPTAIN BROOKS
            How many years would she get for
                         that?

                    CAPTAIN THOMAS
            There's something to be said for no
            bills, medical, which you don't
            have right now, you could get some
            rest, you'd be with Lila, Delia--

                      MICHELLE
                     (standing)
            And we need to get going because we
            only have an hour left to visit
            them at the women's facility.

Mel stands.

                    CAPTAIN THOMAS
            Darling. Everything will work out.

INMATE, EMANUEL DRAGO (30's) walks up behind the
Two Captains as if going towards the vending
machines. He knocks both of the Captains hats off
their heads. Emanuel turns back with a smirk.

                        MEL
            What was that all about?

The Two Captains retrieve their hats from the
floor and put them back on.

                    CAPTAIN THOMAS
            Working on that one.

                    CAPTAIN BROOKS
            All in due time.

Michelle and Mel look at each other nervously.
The two Captains stand.

                    CAPTAIN THOMAS
                (hugging Michelle)
            Don't you two worry about us. Give

our sweet Lila a big hug.

                    CAPTAIN BROOKS
                    (hugging Mel)
               Send them all our love.

                        MICHELLE
                  See you next week.

                    CAPTAIN THOMAS
                      (to Mel)
               Take care of my daughter.

                    CAPTAIN BROOKS
                 And stay out of trouble.

Mel smiles and salutes.

                          MEL
                  It'll be an honor.

Mel and Michelle leave through the prison doors.

EXT. MEN'S CA STATE PRISON/OUTDOOR YARD - LATER

Harold runs bare foot along the dusty field as he
runs around the outer edge along an electric barb
wired fence. Harold runs past a BASKETBALL GAME
between INMATES, Clive in his wheelchair is the
referee, even if the other Inmates haven't asked
him to be.

                    CLIVE MARSHALL
                 (from his wheelchair and
                    the sidelines)
               Man! You a dog! Don't take that
               shit! Chin check the motherfucker!

Harold runs past, waving at the Two Captains and
the other Retired Brigade as they do a little
stretching, up and down touching their toes, a
little yoga and Tai Chi.

                          135

Harold stops and rests next to Crazy Horse and his hard core INKED INMATE FOLLOWERS. Their motto, "bigger is better."
Crazy Horse bench presses two hundred pounds before dropping it to the dust. He looks up and spots Harold watching him with an almost mocking expression.

                CRAZY HORSE
      What you fucking staring at old
                  man?

The other INMATES look up from their punching bags, dumb bells and muscle regime. They gather behind Crazy Horse.

                HAROLD
      I don't understand what good that
           is doing you?

Crazy Horse LAUGHS with the others.

                CRAZY HORSE
      Let me see you try and lift it
           light foot.

                HAROLD
     Oh no... I could never lift it. But
     two hundred pounds? And I'm sorry
     to say son, you walk very strange
         with all that muscle.

Everyone smiles, on their way to LAUGHING but with a cutting expression from Crazy Horse, they all think otherwise.

                CRAZY HORSE
     You think running around the yard
        does anything for you?

                HAROLD
     I'm ninety-one. Heart seems to have
      liked it. Son I don't think you
      could you get around the yard two

time without stopping. The amount
you ate for breakfast, I'll be
visiting you in the ground.

The INMATES are gathering around, basketball game
takes a break, the Two Captains and their
exercise group move towards the potential
challenge match.

                    INMATE 1
        Run the fucking field. Show the old
            Chief he's lost it.

                    INMATE 2
        Better yet. Give him a head start
        and then see who finishes first.

                    HAROLD
        I just ran but I could go around
                one more time.

Inmates start to place bets between each other on
the win.

                    CRAZY HORSE
        I win, I get $100 and whatever I
        want from your meals for the rest
                of the week.

                    HAROLD
        I win. You and your boys train with
                me for a week.

Crazy Horse LAUGHS in disbelief, "like that is
going to happen?" A MOMENT. The bets are going
in. We all know who the Captains and the Retired
boys are voting for. Inmates going for the win on
Crazy Horse. They see money in their horizon.
Harold smiles and slowly gets down on one knee.

                    INMATE 1
        Is he praying for rain or
                something?

137

INMATES are amused, Crazy Horse stands next to Harold.

> CRAZY HORSE
> I'm not going down on my fucking
> knees.

> HAROLD
> That's because you can't.

> EVERYONE
> (cat calls, egging them on)
> Ohhhhhhhh....

Crazy Horse starts to get annoyed. Inmate 1 steps forward.

> INMATE 1
> Muscles verses age.

> INMATE 2
> Brains verses age.

EVERYONE CRACKS up at this.

> CAPTAIN THOMAS
> (to inmates)
> You should reconsider your
> bets...we got a silver medalist--

> CRAZY HORSE
> Can we fucking do this?!

The two Captains step forward.

> CAPTAIN THOMAS
> Two times around the field. No head
> starts.

> CAPTAIN BROOKS
> Runners...on your mark. (a beat)
> Set. Go!

Crazy Horse moves quickly forward. Harold's pace much slower. It's the Prison story version of the "Turtle and the Hare."

First time around, Harold is behind 200 yards. Crazy Horse ego shows on his face, smiling at his boys. His smile turns to a serious expression as a severe side cramp takes away his breath, he can't help but slow. Harold passes him in split seconds at the end of the second lap. Crazy Horse collapses to the ground at the finish line

CHEERS and disbelief on the field. Harold retrieves his prayer stick out of his jumpsuit pocket and places it on his heart.

> CAPTAIN THOMAS
> (grabbing Harold's arms,
> lifting them high in the
> air)
> 1950's Olympic gold medalist folks!

> HAROLD
> Silver.

The crowd goes QUIET. Respect and admiration appear across the Inmates faces.

> HAROLD (CONT'D)
> Light breakfast tomorrow. See you
> all in training.

The MURMURS of disbelief continue as Harold offers Crazy Horse a hand up. Crazy Horse doesn't accept but stands and gives an acceptance smile towards Harold.

YARD - LATER

Single file, the GUARDS recruit the Inmates out of the yard. The two Captains line up with the others before returning to their cells. Emanuel, follows behind the Two Captains knocking the Captains hats off their heads. INMATE 3 grabs the hats off the ground, throws Captain Thomas' hat to Emanuel and they place the stolen hats on their heads.

                    CAPTAIN BROOKS
                    Now what?

                    CAPTAIN THOMAS
            We teach them how to deserve the
                        honor.

The hatless Captains follow the rest of the Inmates inside.

INT. WOMEN'S CA STATE PRISON/VISITING ROOM - 2 WEEKS LATER

CLOSE UP OF PEARLY WHITE DENTURES

Michelle sits with Lila, Delia, Martha and Sara at a table. They are admiring Martha's new set of teeth.

                    MARTHA
            I couldn't do this before on the
            outside. I didn't have to pay a
            cent and I feel like a new woman.

Martha smiles, they all agree that she looks great. Two books sit on the table. The room feels similar to the men's prison. FAMILIES of INMATES sit around tables.

A Vending machines draw the attention of the CHILDREN.
Virginia stands at the front of the line, slowly placing coin by coin into one of the machines.

                    VIRGINIA
            (to the impatient line of
                behind her)
            This country is one big line. Get
                use to it kids!

                        140

The CHILDREN let out a BIG IMPATIENT SIGH.

Back at the table...

                    LILA
              How's Mel?

                  MICHELLE
        At the lawyers today. I think he's
         almost through his horrible
       divorce. He sends you all a hug.

                    LILA
          Your sexual harassment case?

                  MICHELLE
        Chuck dropped it. I had a naked
       picture of him that he sent me by
       text and he titled it "here when
       you want it." I think his wife is
           appreciating it now.

The group of elderly girls at the table move in a
little closer.

              MICHELLE (CONT'D)
           Sorry girls. I erased it.

They may be old but a cute guy naked is still
appreciated.

                   DELIA
          Mel's seems like a good guy.

Everyone at the table nods in agreement.

                  MICHELLE
        I have four mothers trying to set
             me up right now?

They all smile, guilty.

MARTHA
That's becoming our job here.

SARA
Lots of these ladies didn't have
what we had. Drugs, prostitution--

DELIA
They didn't have love and no
parental guidance.

LILA
It feels like I'm back at my
principle job overlooking kids that
just want someone to care.

MICHELLE
I never thought of it that way.

SILENCE.

LILA
Last week, ten more of us arrived.

DELIA
It was a bridge group that didn't
want to lose a few of the girls
that had decided it was time to
give up their financial struggle.
Some of them have money but said
they didn't want to lose their
bridge buddies. So they all held up
Disneyland.

They all look over to a table. One of the bridge
girls, KATIE GRUBIAK (80's) sits with her FAMILY.
We can see the Family is uncomfortable, dressed
immaculate, they have money and never dreamed
they'd be visiting their family member in prison.
Katie smiles and waves at the Lila, Delia and the
group. They all wave back.

SARA
Last week, my grandkids told me my

favorite TV show was talking about
us too.

MARTHA
I overheard CNN had some big wig
therapist on the show analyzing our
crimes. He said our dementia is the
cause of all the crimes.

SARA
That's exactly what they were
discussing on the view. Barbara
Walter's, love that woman, says our
Retirement Brigade won't stop until
our government does something.

MICHELLE
I'm beginning to think she's right.

SARA'S FAMILY, a few CHILDREN enter the visiting
room.

SARA
There they are!

They all notice. Sara and Martha get up from the
table. Martha takes a book off the table.

MARTHA
(to Michelle)
Thanks for the book.

CLOSE UP OF BOOK - VEGETABLE GARDENING IN
SOUTHERN CALIFORNIA

MARTHA (CONT'D)
Kiss my animals. Tell them I miss
them.

Michelle smiles and gets up to give Sara and
Martha a hug.

MICHELLE
Touli and Georgie miss you too.

They fight over who gets the pillow
every night.
(to Sara)
Glad you got your hearing back.

Sara smiles, tapping her left ear hearing aid.

                    SARA
          One of the free perks in this
          place. See you soon sweetie.

Sara takes Martha's arm.

                    SARA (CONT'D)
                    (to Martha)
          Come, I can't wait for you to meet
          my grandson. He loves gardening.

Lila and Delia turn back to Michelle.

                    LILA
          Sweet Sara. Her grandson is a great
          gardener. She has no idea, but his
             pot is better than I've ever
                    smoked.

They all CHUCKLE.

                    MICHELLE
          When's the date of your hip
             surgery?

An uncomfortable SILENCE between Lila and Delia.
Delia stands.

                    DELIA
          I'm going to get us some coffee.

Delia stands and leaves. A MOMENT.

                    LILA
          They aren't going to be doing any
          operation. (a beat) I have late
             stage bone cancer.

144

MICHELLE
I'm so sorry. (a beat) What about
treatment? You can get anything in
here.

Lila shakes her head "no."

LILA
Doctors are giving me nine months
to 2 years. Death penalty is one
thing but never understood how
doctors can estimate a sentence of
death.

MICHELLE
What about chemo? Can they do
anything?

LILA
I don't want the last years of my
life to be fucking bald, barfing
and feeling fucking shitty. For
what? An extra month or so?

Michelle smiles sadly.

MICHELLE
That's the first time I heard you
curse in a long time.

LILA
I don't have the stress anymore.
I'm free.

Lila reaches into her pocket and slides a note to
Michelle.

LILA (CONT'D)
Put it in your pocket, read it
later. I've explained in detail
about Delia's life. She has a
daughter.

Michelle puts the paper in her pocket.

LILA (CONT'D)
She needs to know, Delia is not a
criminal. She might be able to help
us, finish what we started. (a
beat) Can you help me find her?

Delia returns with the coffee. A PRISON CHRISTIAN
MINISTER approaches them at the table.

PRISON MINISTER
Good afternoon. I'd like to
introduce myself.
(to Michelle)
It's so nice to see you again.

Michelle smiles, none of them are exactly into
the "Jesus" recruit at this moment but playing it
up entertains them.

PRISON MINISTER (CONT'D)
(to Lila and Delia)
I wanted to remind you of the bible
study this evening.
(to Lila)
Perhaps I can help you find
strength in this time of need. Did
you know that Jesus began his
earthly ministry with a bold
proclamation. Christ said "good
news for the poor" and "freedom for
the prisoners."

LILA
That's true. We're poor and far
from freedom.

DELIA
We're prisoners?

Michelle smiles, she enjoys watching her friend
have fun with this guy.

PRISON MINISTER
Yes...yes! Yes, you are!

LILA

Jesus speaks to all his children,
even to us wondering souls that are
trapped behind bars.

PRISON MINISTER

Yes!... Oh yes...my child. Come
tonight. Through the love of
Christ, God will save your souls.

The Prison Minister leaves their table and moves
on to the next one. The WHISTLE blows. A GUARD
moves out of his station into the room.

GUARD

Visiting hours are now over. Guests
please proceed to the exit with
your belongings.

Lila, Delia and Michelle stand embrace. Delia
grabs a walker that's been next to the wall and
gives it to Lila.

LILA
(lifting the book off the
table)
Thanks for the book. Shakespeare
was the romantic God, if you ask
me.

DELIA

You should have seen the plays she
put together with the kids back in
her principal days.

MICHELLE

I have no doubt that they probably
put Broadway to shame. See you in a
few weeks.

Michelle watches Delia and Lila join the other
Inmates against the wall. Lila turns from her
walker and mouths the words "Thank you."
Michelle smiles and leaves.

INT. TV HALL - LATER

Captain Thomas and Captain Brooks file into the
room with the other INMATES. They all sit on
chairs waiting for the lights to dim and a movie
to be shown. Emanuel enters with Inmate 3
wearing the Captains hats and sit down. The two
Captains sit behind them.

                    CAPTAIN THOMAS
                (starts singing song by
                    Johnny Nash)
            I can see clearly now the rain is
                        gone...

                    CAPTAIN BROOKS
            I can see all obstacles in my
                        way...

                    CAPTAIN THOMAS
            Gone our dark clouds that had me
                        blind...

        CAPTAIN BROOKS AND CAPTAIN THOMAS
            It's gonna a be a bright (bright),
            bright (bright) sunshiny day...
            It's gonna be a bright (bright)
                    bright--

Emanuel, Inmate 3 and his homeboys turn around
with a look that says "shut up."

        CAPTAIN BROOKS AND CAPTAIN THOMAS
                    (CONT'D)
            Bright...sunshiny day.

                    CAPTAIN THOMAS
            Emanuel...what did you do before
            you came into this place?

                    EMANUEL
            I beat up a cop and--

                    CAPTAIN THOMAS
          What did you do before you beat up
                       a cop?

His homeboys start to LAUGH a little, they know
what he use to do for work.

                       EMANUEL
              Shut the fuck up! At least I
          fucking worked! More than a few of
                     you can say!

                    CAPTAIN THOMAS
             You had kids to feed right?

Emanuel nods "yes", not sure where they are going
with this. A MOMENT.

                       EMANUEL
            Garbage... I collected garbage.

The homeboys smile again but decide to back off.
It's not good to go against Emanuel.

                    CAPTAIN THOMAS
            Someone's trash becomes someone
                  else's treasures.

                       EMANUEL
           Fucking right! I made some fucking
             cool shit for my kid out of the
           trash. Skateboard, bicycle...I even
               found an old electric model
           airplane, was so fucking broken up
           but I found a way to fix it...you
           know? Little remote control thing,
              never seen the kid so fucking
                        happy.

                    CAPTAIN THOMAS
           I was the captain on a flight from
          New York to London back in my day.
          One of the engines failed and I had
          to control and then land that thing

manually in unfriendly skies.
Doesn't matter what type of
aircraft it is, a 747 or a model
toy...it's a work of genius that
keeps anything up in the air.

Emanuel and his boys are impressed.

> EMANUAL
> (to Captain Brooks)
> What about you?

> CAPTAIN BROOKS
> A bottle of whisky took me off
> course a little.

> CAPTAIN THOMAS
> But he was a fine Captain of the
> sea and he has a fucking great
> voice.

Emanuel and the boys smile.

> CAPTAIN THOMAS (CONT'D)
> You want to earn those hats? I can
> teach you boys how to fly.

They LAUGH at this and then realize the Captains
are serious.

> INMATE 3
> Fuck yeah!

They are all interested but wait to get the "Go"
from Emanuel.

> EMANUEL
> Seems fucking impossible.

> CAPTAIN THOMAS
> That's what they said when you made
> the things for your kid.

A MOMENT. Lights begin to dim in the room. Emanuel's expression tells us he's in. They all turn around to watch the evening movie.

> CAPTAIN BROOKS
> I think I can make it now, the pain
> is gone...

> CAPTAIN THOMAS
> All of the bad feelings have a
> disappeared...

Emanuel and Inmate 3 look at each other before removing the Captains hats off their heads and tossing them back onto the Captains laps. The two Captains smile and place their hats back on their heads.

INT. WOMEN'S CALIFORNIA STATE PRISON/MEETING HALL - SAME TIME

Inmates fill the chairs, some looking very uninterested. Chrystal (the Inmate that knocked Sara's breakfast tray over) sits in front of Lila and Delia.

The Prison Minister is at the front of the room with his bible.

PRISON MINISTER
Matthew 15:4. The fifth commandment. For God said 'Honor thy father and thy mother' Anyone who curses their father or mother, is to be put to death.'

Lila raises her hand. The Prison Minister points to her.

> LILA
> Over thirty years ago, I was a
> principle at a school in downtown
> Los Angeles. Children would come
> into my office when they needed to

talk. Most of their stories were
about the problems they were having
at home. (a beat) I recall, one
little girl, she told me she was
afraid of her father and that he
took his anger out on her and the
mother. Maybe there are a few other
woman in here that can relate to
what I'm speaking of.

More than a few Inmates nod their heads "yes."

                    LILA (CONT'D)
One day she came into my office
with tears streaming down her face,
in her hands lay the most beautiful
butterfly I think I have ever seen.

Chrystal turns around and stares at Lila and
Delia before turning back to look at the front.
The story is about her.

                    LILA (CONT'D)
She had seen one of her classmates
catch it and in the course of
catching it, the wing was broken
and it was dying.

                    PRISON MINISTER
It would be welcomed in heaven, to
the Lord almighty--

All the Inmates "SHHHHHH" the Priest to shut-up.

                    LILA
This little girl could not
understand why the most beautiful
thing she ever seen had to die such
a tragic death. I hugged her and
tried to explain life wasn't always
what we wanted it to be. (a beat)
The next day, I was told the little
girl's father had murdered her
mother. I never saw the little girl

at my school again. How can a
little child honor her father when
he took one of the most beautiful
things away from her?

SILENCE in the room. Lila and Delia stand.

                    LILA (CONT'D)
I'm starting a book club and
creative writing class. We will
explore stories of comedy, tragedy,
politics, romance and hate. What I
believe is the ingredients of life.
Everyone has a story, and I believe
there probably isn't one woman in
here that hasn't experienced the
broken wing of a butterfly.

A MOMENT.

                    PRISON MINISTER
What a lovely story. Let's all bow
our heads in prayer...as we...

Time is up, the Inmates are excitedly talking
amongst themselves as they move towards the GUARD
waiting by the door. Chrystal remains seated,
wiping her teared face. Lila places her hand on
Chrystal's shoulder as Delia and Lila follow the
other Inmates out the door. Chrystal follows.

                    PRISON MINISTER (CONT'D)
God bless you...thank you everyone!

The Inmates are too busy talking about their
stories to hear his good-byes.

MONTAGE OF SHOTS

EXT. WOMEN CA STATE PRISON/MARTHA'S GARDEN -
MORNING

In the baron prison yard next to the visiting
room, Virginia

passes out shovels to the Inmates.
Sara organizes a few Inmates the unloading of fresh soil, seeds and fertilizer off the back of a delivery truck. Martha directs the younger Inmates where to begin the trenches.

EXT. MEN'S CA STATE PRISON/HAROLD'S TRACK TEAM - AFTERNOON

Crazy Horse and his other Homeboys have removed their shoes and stand in a group listening to Harold. Sweat drenches their tired bodies, but they're thriving on it. Harold is teaching them how to use the coordination of arms and legs as if they were jumping a hurdle.

INT. MEN'S CA STATE PRISON/TV ROOM - EVENING

Captain Thomas is sitting in a chair facing the group holding a "Playboy" magazine up as if he were reading it, but his arms straight out in front of him. Captain Brooks stands behind the chair; his eyes have been distracted by the magazine.

A diagram of an airplane cockpit on a chalkboard is behind them.

CLOSE UP OF A DIAGRAM OF PLANE DASHBOARD. ALTITUDE READERS, CONTROL DISPLAY, RADAR DISPLAY and NAVIGATION CONTROLS.
Takeoff sequencing is written underneath. V1- decision speed/ VR- Rotation speed/ V2- Speed that produces best angle to climb.

Captain Thomas pushes the imaginary throttle forward with his right hand, he holds the magazine in his left hand as if it was the control wheel.

                    CAPTAIN THOMAS
                    Check power.

SILENCE. No response. Captain Brooks Co-piloting skills have been distracted by the dirty magazine in front of him.

> CAPTAIN THOMAS (CONT'D)
> CHECK POWER!

> CAPTAIN BROOKS
> Ah...sorry! But let me borrow that magazine after you're done with it.

Captain Brooks pretends to check throttle and speeds.

> CAPTAIN THOMAS
> Ready for takeoff. Three speeds have been determined. V-1, V-R and V-2.

Captain Brooks is shaking Captain Thomas' chair, his plane is picking up speed.

> CAPTAIN BROOKS
> 100 knots.

Emanual and half the group of Inmates sit in chairs holding a magazine or book. A good portion of them are holding an months issue of "Playboy" magazine, the other half of the room stand behind the chairs. Chairs are shaking, take off is about to happen for all of them.

> CAPTAIN BROOKS AND ALL CO-PILOTS
> V-1! (a beat) Rotate!

> CAPTAIN THOMAS
> (imaginary yoke)
> Captains! Pull back on the yoke.

Captain Brooks tilts Captain Thomas' chair back on it's hind legs, as if the nose of the plane was going up into the sky. Emanual and the other Inmates copycat the Captains. Big smiles across their faces.

CHEERS FROM EVERYONE. They made it to take-off.

                    EMANUAL
          (chair back, he's taking
                    off)
          Mile high club! Here we fucking
                    come.

INT. WOMEN'S CA STATE PRISON/MEETING HALL - SAME
TIME

Lila reads from SHAKESPEARE'S "Romeo and Juliet,"
at the front of the room. She has the attention
of a large group of Inmates. The Retired Brigade
has joined; everyone holds some type of paper or
book with a pen in their hands.

                    LILA
                  (Juliet)
          From nine to twelve is three long
          hours, yet she has not come. Had
          she affections of warm youthful
          blood, she'd be swift in motion as
          a ball, my words would bandy her to
          my sweet love and his to me. But
          old folks many feign as they were
          dead, unwieldy, slow, heavy and
                  pale as lead.

Lila looks up from her book. Chrystal, Sara,
Virginia and few and over half the room raise
their hands eagerly. Lila points to Virginia.

                  VIRGINIA
          That Juliet is making fun of the
          old lady nurse. I say she needs her
                bottom spanked!

Everyone LAUGHS. Lila points to Chrystal.

                  CHRYSTAL
          The nurse loves Juliet and she
          understands how much Juliet loves

Romeo. The nurse is risking her
life by taking the letter to him.

Lila holds out the book to the next Inmate in
line to read. They continue the story of "Romeo
and Juliet."

INT. MICHELLE'S APARTMENT

Michelle stares at the TV. Touli and Georgie
sleep on the couch next to her. Mel joins her
from the kitchen with two glasses of wine. Mel
turns up the volume on the TV.

CLOSE UP OF TV SCREEN. IT'S THE STEPHEN COLBERT
SHOW.

> STEPHEN COLBERT
> Please join me in a round of
> applause for Kamilla Harrison. The
> First Woman Governor of the state
> of California!

LOUD APPLAUSE as KAMILLA HARRISON WALKS OUT ON
STAGE.

Michelle shakes her head in disbelief.

> MICHELLE
> There she is. Delia's daughter.

> MEL
> You think Chuck is going to pull
> through for you?

> MICHELLE
> He said he'll meet me. We'll see
> tomorrow.

BACK TO THE TV SCREEN

The Governor takes a seat next to STEPHEN
COLBERT's desk.

                    STEPHEN COLBERT
            Welcome to our show. Right off the
            bat! Let's talk about something
            that you mentioned to me earlier
                     back stage...

                    KAMILLA HARRISON
              Ah...The Retirement Brigade.

                    STEPHEN COLBERT
            Your grandparents robbed any banks
                      lately?"

The AUDIENCE LAUGHS, so does Kamilla.

                    KAMILLA HARRISON
            But really...it's a very serious
            problem and something needs to be
                   done about it.

                    STEPHEN COLBERT
             But I heard that prisons are
            improving since the old guys are in
            there turning our prisoners around--

                    KAMILLA HARRISON
            That's true. Repeated crime rates
              are dropping but the banks are
            still being robbed by elderly first
              time offenders. We have to
            implement a new health care system
             that includes full medical and
                   assisted living.

                    STEPHEN COLBERT
            When you're on the inside you get
                 everything for free...

                    KAMILLA HARRISON
             And good law abiding American
            citizens have to pay out of pocket.

                    STEPHEN COLBERT
             I agree. It's the very least we

should be doing.

AUDIENCE CLAPS in agreement.

> STEPHEN COLBERT (CONT'D)
> Did you hear about the old guy who
> used a parachute to rob the 7-11
> last week?

EXT. BANK OF AMERICA - NEXT DAY- MORNING

Michelle sits in her car in the parking lot.
Chuck pulls up next to her, gets out of his car
and gets in next to Michelle in her passenger
seat. An AWKWARD MOMENT.

> MICHELLE
> Any luck?

> CHUCK HARRIS
> No... Hi Chuck? Thanks for meeting
> me?

A MOMENT

> MICHELLE
> Sorry. (a beat) Any luck?

Chuck gives her a piece of paper.

> CHUCK HARRIS
> I didn't like many of my sisters
> friends growing up but Kamilla was
> one cool girl. They still call each
> other every year on their birthday.

> MICHELLE
> I'm so glad I remembered you
> telling me they were high school
> friends.

> CHUCK
> You remember everything. (a beat)

You can have your job back, if you
want it.

Michelle shakes her head "no." A MOMENT.

                    MICHELLE
        Thanks for the offer though.

Chuck gets out of the car and leans back in
through the window.

                  CHUCK HARRIS
        Whoever gets you, is one lucky man.

Michelle watches Chuck walk into the bank. She
looks at the paper and dials her cell phone. It
rings.

              KAMILLA HARRISON (O.S)
                  Good morning.

                    MICHELLE
                  (into phone)
        Hello... good morning. My name is
        Michelle Thomas. You don't know me
             but I need to give you some
                information regarding the
        Retirement Brigade. You may recall
        hearing the name of Delia Zamora.
        She was one of the elderly woman
        involved with the The First Lady
                 Bank Robbery.

                KAMILLA HARRISON
        Yes...I remember this name.

A MOMENT. Michelle takes a deep breath before...

                    MICHELLE
        Delia Zamora is your birth mother.
             (a beat) She worked for your
        parents when she was nineteen...she
        became pregnant. (a beat) It was
        your father's child. Delia left her

job as your parents' housekeeper and
later because of no work and no
money, she got into some trouble
with the law. (a beat) She gave up
her daughter to the father. Your
mother, as you know her, raised you
like her own. And because your
father was a Superior Court judge,
the story was hidden and your life
as you know it (a beat) is not
completely the truth.

SILENCE ON THE OTHER LINE.

                    MICHELLE (CONT'D)
                    Hello?

                    KAMILLA HARRISON
          Is this some kind of a prank?

                    MICHELLE
          No. I swear it's the truth and--

                    KAMILLA HARRISON
          I don't know how you got my
          personal number but...please don't
                    call me again.

CLICK! Kamilla hangs up the phone.

Michelle is defeated. She dials Mel's number.

                    MEL (O.S.)
                    And? How did it go?

Tears begin to fall down Michelle's cheeks.

                    MICHELLE
          Why does life have to be so
                    difficult?

MONTAGE OF SHOTS/THREE MONTHS LATER

EXT. WOMEN'S CA STATE PRISON/MARTHA'S GARDEN -
AFTERNOON

The desolate yard that was once a dirt mound is
now a picture of green life. Tomato plants,
cabbage, especially the raspberry bushes are the
main attraction of the INMATES visiting CHILDREN.
Martha pulls a carrot out of the ground and gives
Sara and her GRANDCHILD. Proud of their efforts,
the Inmates appear to be happier. Where there is
growth there's hope.

INT. MEN'S CA STATE PRISON/TV ROOM - EVENING

Captain Thomas and Captain Brooks stand at the
front of the room; they have blindfolds on.
Emanual and the other Inmates stand around them.
Even the GUARDS seem to be in on it. Emanuel
removes the blindfolds.

In front of the Captains stand a work of art. It
is a COCKPIT OF AN AIRPLANE, assembled from
discarded parts of an aircraft. Two old airplane
seats are waiting for the Captains to sit down.

The Captains sit down in complete awe of what
they are looking at.

> EMANUAL
> (to Captain Brooks)
> You'll get your boat Captains
> bridge next. I've already been
> working on the plans.

Captain Brooks smiles. He's genuinely happy for
Captain Thomas at this moment. Tears in his eyes,
Captain Thomas moves the throttle back and forth
with his right hand.

> EMANUAL (CONT'D)
> Shit man! What did you teach us?

Captain Thomas and Captain Brooks look at them blankly.

                    EVERYONE
              Seat belt!

They all LAUGH as the Captains put on their seat belts.

                 CAPTAIN THOMAS
              How did you do this?

Everyone looks at Emanual, insinuating he's a the one behind it all.

                    EMANUAL
              Everyone helped.

                     GUARD
           Including me. I got friends in high
                     places.

                    EMANUAL
           We want to take a pilot's exam. We
           know it means nothing out there...
                (hitting his heart)
           In here (a beat) it means
                   everything.

Captain Thomas looks at Captain Brooks. They smile proudly.

EXT. MEN'S CA STATE PRISON/OUTDOOR YARD - AFTERNOON

Crazy Horse warms up with five other Inmates. Harold watches over them, today he holds a small white pillow under his arm. Crazy Horse and the other Inmates prepare to race.

                   INMATE 4
              It's a 400-meter dash. One time
                 around the field.

A crowd of Inmates, including the Captains and Retirement Brigade place their bets on the race. The runners begin to line up behind a line drawn in the dirt.

> CRAZY HORSE
> (having fun)
> You not running this race?
> Gonna take a little rest with your
> pillow?

> HAROLD
> Feeling my age today.

> CRAZY HORSE
> You? No fucking way.

Harold gives Crazy Horse his prayer stick. Crazy Horse is taken aback by this gesture. Harold begins to walk towards the sidelines to watch the race from a chair.

> CRAZY HORSE (CONT'D)
> ...Thanks. (a beat) I've been
> meaning to ask you. You never did
> tell me your Native name?

Harold turns and with happy contentment sits down in the chair.

> HAROLD
> Sitting Bull.

Crazy Horse smiles and kneels down onto one knee, holding the prayer stick as if it were a baton. The competitors take their mark.

Crazy Horse looks up at Harold one last time. Their eyes meet and they smile.

> INMATE 4
> Runners. On your mark. Set. Go!

Crazy Horse takes off, prayer stick in hand.

INT. WOMEN'S CA STATE PRISON/VISITING ROOM- SAME
TIME

Lila sits in a wheelchair at the front of the
room, her health deteriorating. Delia, Michelle,
Mel and Mr. Mizrahi sit next to her. An Audience
of FAMILY MEMBERS and FRIENDS watch a
performance. A few tears from the INMATES
SUPPORTERS as they watch the final act of
SHAKESPEARE'S "Romeo and Juliet."

At the front of the room, Chrystal is "JULIET."
She sits next to "ROMEO" played by another INMATE
lying asleep on the floor. Chrystal has lifted
Romeo's dagger into the air...

                    CHRYSTAL/JULIET
                This is thy sheath;
                 (stabs herself)
            There rust, and let me die.

Juliet falls on Romeo and dies.

EXT. MEN'S CA STATE PRISON/OUTDOOR YARD - SAME
TIME

APPLAUSE as Crazy Horse wine the 400-meter dash.
He lifts his prayer stick in the air and looks
over for a response from his coach. The APPLAUSE
of the win dies down to SILENCE as Crazy Horse's
demeanor changes. He walks towards Harold.

Harold sits slumped over on his chair, his pillow
lay on his lap. His head found his pillow, just
how he wanted it.

INT. WOMEN'S CA STATE PRISON/VISITING ROOM - SAME
TIME

APPLAUSE dies down as Delia steps forward from
the line of "Romeo and Juliet" INMATE ACTORS.

                    DELIA
        I speak on behalf of our director
           and friend Lila Simmons.

LOUD APPLAUSE from the entire room, even the
GUARDS. Lila smiles weakly from her wheelchair,
thanking everyone.

                 DELIA (CONT'D)
             (taking a deep breath)
        Lila would like to thank each and
        everyone of you for all your hard
        work and efforts. In the time we
       put together this play, we have all
       grown as people and become one. We
          have shared our own stories of
          grief, hardship, life's mistakes
          and our dreams of what we want in
          life don't seem as far away as we
         once thought. We...all of us...can
            be anything we want to be. We
          proved that here today. But saying
          all that...Lila Simmons. Thank you
          from all of us. Your love... shows
          through with everything you have...

Delia slows in her speech. Governor Kamilla
Harrison has just entered the room. The Audience
turns to follow Delia's stare.
A Guard escorts Kamilla up to the front of the
room. Delia's shocked stare, turns into tears as
the Governor stands before her.

                KAMILLA HARRISON
        Today seemed the perfect time to
            meet (a beat) my mother.

A MOMENT. The AUDIENCE is trying to figure out
the story.
Lila places her hand on Michelle's knee. Their
efforts and wishes have just been answered.
Delia smiles through her tears.

> DELIA
> Happy Birthday my little girl.

Delia and her daughter embrace in tears for the
first time in over 45 years.

INT. LILA AND DELIA'S JAIL CELL - EVENING

Delia helps Lila out of her wheel chair and into
her bottom bunk. Delia stands and removes a small
picture that has been taped to the wall. Delia
sits on the bed and gives it to Lila.

Lila weakly smiles admiring the photo as she
always has.

> LILA
> I never gave birth to a child but I
> feel like I raised a thousand.

Lila passes the photo back to Delia as she nods
in agreement through her tears beginning to
stream down her face.

> LILA (CONT'D)
> You're not mad at me for finding
> her?

Delia shakes her head no.

A GUARD passes the cell and peaks in through the
bars. Delia stands and walks up to the bars.

> THE GUARD
> (compassionately)
> How's she doing?

Delia smiles sadly and shakes her head. Lila is
close to death.

> THE GUARD (CONT'D)
> If you need anything, I'm on the
> night shift. Let me know.

Delia returns back to Lila's bed. Lila passes the picture back to Delia.

> LILA
> It's all going...to be...ok now. We
> did it. We really did...

Lila drifts out of consciousness. Delia wipes her tear stained face and looks at the picture.

Adjusting a small white pillow under Lila's frail head, Delia lay next to her and spoons her as if she were spooning a child. The picture drops from her hand next to them as Delia falls asleep with her friend for the last time.

CLOSE UP OF PICTURE IS OF DELIA (20) AND KAMILLA (baby). Delia has just given birth and she's lying in a hospital bed, spooning her sleeping new born.

INT. MEN'S CA STATE PRISON/VISITING ROOM - ONE YEAR LATER

The Two Captains sit with Michelle, Mel and Mr. Mizrahi. The Retirement Brigade and Inmates mood is more upbeat. Visiting hours are more of a party than a downer now. Hope fills the air. Across the table are photographs of the construction of a Retirement center.

> MICHELLE
> What do you boys think of the name
> "Two Captains Plaza."

The two Captains smile wide and turn to Mr. Mizrahi.

> CAPTAIN THOMAS
> We can't thank you enough for
> making this happen.

Michelle puts her arm around Mr. Mizrahi.

> MR. MIZRAHI
> What else am I going to do with
> fifty million dollars?

> MEL
> This thing has gone crazy. Bill
> Gates, Buffet and get this, (a
> beat) Donald Trump. Privately
> funding their own non profit
> retirement centers.

> CAPTAIN BROOKS
> Well...I'll be damned! Mr Trump?
> Did someone finally tell him to
> change his hairstylist?

> CAPTAIN THOMAS
> Sounds like it. Now he's thinking
> straight.

They all LAUGH.

> MICHELLE
> All you and your friends ready for
> next week?

> CAPTAIN THOMAS
> Nervous as hell.

> CAPTAIN BROOKS
> We all are.

> CAPTAIN THOMAS
> This all goes down, we got a long
> list of friends that will be
> looking for jobs when they get out
> of this place.

> CAPTAIN BROOKS
> We gotta make sure we get the
> kitchen crew we got in there right
> now. Damn! Those meals are better

than any home cooking I've ever
tasted.

Michelle and Mel are impressed.

                    MICHELLE
          That's why I thought you looked
          like you gained a couple of pounds.

                    MEL
          Governor Harrison has been all over
          the news lately. She has the entire
          state and country on her side.

                    CAPTAIN THOMAS
          We've come a long way since "The
          First Lady Bank Robbery."

They all CHUCKLE but then remember their friend
Lila. A MOMENT.

                    CAPTAIN THOMAS (CONT'D)
          I'm going to really miss that Lila.

They all agree.

                    CAPTAIN BROOKS
          Next week, this state will be sunny
          California as we knew it.

                    MICHELLE
          And if it doesn't work out the way
          we want?

                    CAPTAIN THOMAS
          It will. Lila will be there with
          us.

They all smile and agree. The WHISTLE blows.
Visiting hours are over. They stand and hug each
other goodbye.

As Michelle, Mel and Mr, Mizrahi begin to leave.

MR. MIZRAHI
It's a long trip back. I'll use the
boys room. Meet you at your car.

EXT. MEN'S CA STATE PRISON/PARKING LOT

Michelle and Mel's lean against the hood of the
mini-van, they look out over the vast concrete
parking lot and stark prison facilities. A cement
curb surrounds a perfect little patch of grass
sticks out like a sore thumb in the middle of
the parking lot.

MICHELLE
Who do think waters that?

Mel walks over to the patch of grass and stands
in the middle of it. He looks down and then up to
the sky, as if the answer might be a rain cloud
right over head.

MEL
(referring to the grass)
When I was a kid this is all I
knew. My dad would come home from
a cruise. He'd take me out for a
round of catch, he'd get me a soft
serve if I caught the ball ten
times in a row...Our grass was
greener then the Beaver Cleaver
family. (a beat) Boy did I go
wrong. My wife was obsessed with
having a child, we were prepared
for twenty years, why do you think
I have a mini-van?

MICHELLE
It's not your fault that she didn't
get pregnant.

MEL
Yes, it is! I mean...I never got
tested because I knew if I was

171

infertile than she would have left
me. But she left anyway, pregnant
with my best friend's child. What
I'm trying to say...is I don't
think we can have kids but I'm
really a good guy and I actually
didn't think I could trust a woman
again and... well now I do...

MICHELLE
When I was young, my dad would come
back from a trip. I'd always ask
him how was it to fly way up there.
(a beat) He'd lie down on his back,
stick his feet in the air, I'd put
my tummy on his feet, grab onto his
hands and he'd press me up. I'd let
go. (a beat) I was flying. (a
beat) I will always remember the
sound of my mother giggling from
the kitchen sink.

Mel gets down on his back on the patch of grass
and bends his legs. Looking up at Michelle.

MICHELLE (CONT'D)
What are you doing?

MEL
Get on.

Michelle LAUGHS incredulously.

MICHELLE
Damn it girl. Get on.

Michelle lay her hips on his feet, holds his
hands and he presses her up into the air. She
takes her hands off his feet and spreads them out
like wings.

MEL
Michelle. Will...?

                    MICHELLE
        Hurry up and ask me because I'm
           going to barf all over you.

                      MEL
                  Be my wife?

                    MICHELLE
           Only if you keep the mini van.

Mr. Mizrahi moves in closer, CLAPPING. He's been
watching the whole time.

                   MR. MIZRAHI
        Best proposal I've seen in my life.

Mr. Mizrahi gets into the minivan and Michelle
collapses on Mel LAUGHING.
They kiss passionately.

EXT. MEN'S CA STATE PRISON/PARKING LOT - ONE WEEK
LATER

News helicopters circle high overhead. The
parking lot is jam packed with News trucks, LAPD,
Security Personal and FANS OF THE RETIREMENT
BRIGADE.

Michelle, Mel and Mr. Mizrahi find their place
for the best view, waiting for the much
anticipated morning. A BLACK LIMO comes into view
escorted by the POLICE. The CROWD CLAPS
WILDLY as the limo parks next to the patch of
grass that Mel proposed to Michelle on. The
Governor of California, SECRETARY OF STATE and
other OFFICIALS step out of the limo and move to
the patch of grass where a microphone has been
preset. EVERYONE CLAPS WILDLY.

The CROWD OF SUPPORTERS CLAPPING becomes more
climatic as a YELLOW BUS drives down the long
dusty road leading to the men's prison. We see

the wording on the bus "WOMEN'S CALIFORNIA STATE PRISON."

The Yellow bus comes to a stop in front of the prison.

DEAD SILENCE in the crowd. Anticipation...

CLANK. A GUARD opens the MEN'S PRISON DOOR simultaneously with the yellow bus. The men and the women join each other from The Retirement Brigade for the first time in four years. They line up along the walls of the prison, all wearing their prison jumpsuits and carrying a small white pillow in their hands. FIFTY ELDERLY PRISONERS stand and face their country.

SILENCE. It appears they are all waiting for someone.

In the distance, a man dressed in leathers flies down the dusty road on his Harley Davidson. The crowd steps back as the motorcyclist makes his way to the patch of grass and parks his bike.

The crowd thinks he a celebrity as he removes his sunglasses, helmet and leather jacket. Judge Green grabs his suit jacket out of his top case and puts it on like he's alone in his bedroom. He then acknowledges the world like a cool cat and joins the Governor and the others on the patch of grass.

Governor Harrison does a once over of Judge Green.

> KAMILLA HARRISON
> Nice ride.

> JUDGE GREEN
> I have an extra helmet.

They both smile. They've been working together on this for four years, they know each other well.

But now it's time for business. Judge Green and Governor Harrison step forward towards the microphone.

Listing off the pardoned prisoners, Captain Brooks name is listed off, he smiles, looks up to the heavens and places his right hand on his heart.

> CAPTAIN BROOKS
> For you Lila...
> (singing Anthem)
> O say can you see by the dawn's
> early light. What so proudly we
> hailed at the twilight's last
> gleaming.

Captain Thomas places his hand on his heart and joins CAPTAIN BROOKS AND CAPTAIN THOMAS whose broad stripes and bright stars through the perilous fight,O'er the ramparts we watched, were so gallantly streaming?

AMERICAN ANTHEM continues...

SERIES OF SHOTS OF THE AMERICAN PUBLIC, THE INMATES INSIDE PRISON WATCHING LIVE COVERAGE ON THE TV, NEWS CREWS ETC
PLACING THEIR HANDS ON THEIR HEART. MEL PUTS HIS ARM AROUND MICHELLE, THEY DID IT. FEELING THE PRIDE OF AMERICA AS THE GOVERNOR CONTINUES TO LIST OFF THE PARDONED NAMES.

> CAPTAIN BROOKS AND CAPTAIN THOMAS
> (CONT'D)
> 'T is the star-spangled banner, O!
> long may it wave. O'er the land of
> the free and the home of the brave.

Fifty names have been pardoned. The Crowd goes wild as the Retired Brigade throw the white pillows into the sky. A victory that will never be forgotten.

APPLAUSE and the SOUND of a LARGE GANG OF HARLEY DAVIDSON'S are heard in the distance.

Judge Green already in his leather jacket, places his helmet on his head. Straddling his Harley, he smiles at the Governor with a wink of an eye. Sunglasses back on, he joins his motorcycle group as they wait on the outskirts of the prison.

> GOVERNOR HARRISON
> (to Secretary of State)
> That's one cool cat.

The CROWD goes crazy with admiration as Judge Green leaves the scene.

INT. MICHELLE'S APARTMENT/MORNING - ONE YEAR LATER

Michelle, dressed in her running gear, kneels, throwing up into her toilet bowl. She leans on the sink looking down at the counter.

CLOSE UP OF PREGNANCY TEST... POSITIVE.

She looks at herself in the mirror.

> MICHELLE
> You've got to be kidding me?

She takes the pregnancy test and leaves.

EXT. TWO CAPTAINS RETIREMENT PLAZA - LATER

Michelle jogs up and stops to look up at the sign.

CLOSE UP OF SIGN READS TWO CAPTAINS PLAZA.

Michelle goes inside.

INT. TWO CAPTAINS PLAZA - CONTINUOUS

Michelle enters catching Mr. Mizrahi standing
behind the Receptionist that we know from the
previous Plaza. Mr. Mizrahi has been having a
morning visit, and also has a great
view of her cleavage from behind her with his
binoculars.
The front desk has been designed to look like a
bridge of a boat. Emanual sits on the floor,
assembling an old boat wheel to the bow of the
boat.

                    MR. MIZRAHI
          Ah...Good morning dear. Welcome
                      aboard.

                    MICHELLE
            Wow! It's magnificent!

Emanuel smiles proud. Mr. Mizrahi points towards
the dining room.

                    MR. MIZRAHI
          Breakfast is served. Eggs Benedict
                     Tuesday!

Michelle smiles and leaves towards the dining
room.

DINING ROOM

Michelle enters the room and watches the beauty
of all their efforts. Touli and Georgie still
sleep their bed in the corner of the room. Martha
places a bowl of food down next to them. Delia
sits with Sara, Rick and Clive at a table
discussing the Governor. Crazy Horse helps an
Elderly Man sit at the table. Chrystal pours some
coffee into one of the Residents cups. Captain
Thomas, Captain Brooks and Mel enter the room in
deep discussion. The rest of the staff and

residents look familiar from the men and women prisons. They all see Michelle and greet her with a smile and wave.

Captain Thomas, Captain Brooks and Mel enter the room in deep discussion. They see Michelle and walk over and embrace her.

>   MICHELLE
>   What are you guys so serious about?

>   MEL
>   Guess?

Michelle rolls her eyes and puts her hands on both of the Captains shoulders.

>   MICHELLE
>   We don't care if it's on land, air
>   or sea but we just want the wedding
>   to be simple.

>   CAPTAIN THOMAS
>   We need to be organized.

>   CAPTAIN BROOKS
>   No last minute surprises.

Michelle smiles mischievously, knowing what she's about to show them is definitely going to be a surprise.
She pulls out the pregnancy test and gives it to Mel. The Two Captains and Mel stare at it for a MOMENT.

>   CAPTAIN THOMAS
>   Is that a rectal thermometer?

>   CAPTAIN BROOKS
>   Is that what their giving for
>   wedding presents nowadays?

Mel grabs Michelle and hugs her like this gift has just given him a whole new life.

                  MICHELLE
        I'll be back in half an hour.

Michelle starts to leave and turns back with a smile.

             MICHELLE (CONT'D)
          Love you guys.

Michelle leaves Mel with the task of telling the Two Captains they're going to be grandparents.

Michelle turns back and smiles with a wave to Mr. Mizrahi before leaving. Reception phone RINGS. Mr. Mizrahi waves to Michelle and answers the phone at the same time.

            MR. MIZRAHI
           (into phone)
     It's a beautiful day at the Plaza!

EXT. BEACH - MOMENTS LATER

Michelle jogs along the beach and slows to a stop. Removing her shoes and shirt, A LOUD POLICE SIREN interrupts the perfect morning skinny dip. Michelle continues quickly to remove her shorts. She runs butt naked towards the ocean and dives in. She turns back towards shore.

BEACH CONTROL SUV comes to a halt next to her pile of clothes. Mr. Beach Control, the same guy that gave her a ticket years ago, storms out of his car with his microphone.

          MR. BEACH PATROL
    There is no nudity on the beach.
   You need to come out of the water
   and put on your clothes. (a beat)
    I repeat! Come out of the...

(O.S.) GIGGLES just down the beach.

Mr. Beach Patrol looks down the beach. Twenty elderly known as "THE RETIRED STREAKERS" are on their way into the ocean for their morning skinny dip.

Mr. Beach Control expression on his face turns to "Oh shit!"

FROM THE OCEAN

Michelle smiles at Mr. Beach Patrol's early morning dilemma.

MICHELLE
Better call for back up.

Michelle swims towards her friends to say good morning.

FADE TO BLACK

SLATE: There is no endings Only beginnings.

THE END

www.ingramcontent.com/pod-product-compliance
Lightning Source LLC
Chambersburg PA
CBHW050346030726
47503CB00008B/2648